THE UNIVERSA
VAMPIRISM: FAC

It was a horrible crime. David ᴅᴠ_____, _____, had been found dead in his office and a $400,000 string of pearls missing. So in stepped Police Commissioner Charles Ethredge and his ace crime fighter, Detective-Lieutenant Peters. It was their job to investigate what looked like, at least superficially, an ordinary case of murder. However, the facts in the case just didn't seem to add up:

1. Eichelman had apparently bled to death.
2. His body showed no wounds.
3. No escape route was possible for the assailant, the room having been securely locked from the inside.

Even worse, incidents after the crime were proving to be just as puzzling:

1. Eichelman's body disappeared from the morgue.
2. Later Eichelman was seen alive by a security officer whom Eichelman had loudly admonished.
3. More "dead" bodies began turning up, first alive, then dead again.
4. Eichelman's body was found—dead again—along the side of a road, dead for at least 36 hours.

In all this a prime suspect appeared to be emerging, a strange foreign fellow named Count Woerz. It was up to Ethredge and Peters to determine whether Woerz was innocent or guilty, normal or abnormal, natural or supernatural…

FOR A COMPLETE SECOND NOVEL, TURN TO PAGE 87

CAST OF CHARACTERS

COMMISSIONER CHARLES EHTREDGE
As a stalwart Police Commissioner, he was credited with solving many crimes of both a normal and abnormal nature—but what about crimes of a "supernatural" nature?

COUNT LEOPOLD WOERZ
This extremely wealthy, satanically handsome, ultimately charismatic Hungarian nobleman came from a very old family—a family with a horribly dark secret.

DETECTIVE-LIEUTENANT PETERS
Being quick and smart had saved his hide many times during his long career as a homicide detective; but how would those skills hold up when pitted against the powers of the living dead?

MARY ROBERTS
Very pretty and always soft-spoken and quiet, yet she always seemed to find nifty little clues for her detective boyfriend and often found herself the target his criminal adversaries.

DAVID EICHELMAN
As an experienced jewel merchant, he thought he was as good a judge of men as he was a judge of the jewels he procured for his clients—but he soon found out just how wrong he was!

LOOT OF THE VAMPIRE

By
THORP McCLUSKY

ARMCHAIR FICTION
PO Box 4369, Medford, Oregon 97504

*For more information about Armchair Books and products, visit our
website at…*

www.armchairfiction.com

Or email us at…

armchairfiction@yahoo.com

CHAPTER ONE
The Pearl Necklace

TWO men sat facing each other across David Eichelman's graceful, kidney-shaped desk. They sat in a room of richness, a room in which every item of furniture, every etching, every rug, every softly toned lamp, reflected impeccable taste. David Eichelman was a jewel merchant of international repute.

The hour was immediately after twilight. The jeweler still wore the conservative business suit into which he invariably changed, each noon, at exactly twelve; his visitor was already in evening dress…

On the desk, between the two men, its leather cover thrown open, lay a small oblong box. Within the box four hundred thousand dollars in matched, strung pearls softly shimmered.

The visitor was speaking.

"You understand my reasons, Eichelman, for making this appointment after your regular hours. The young woman— you understand—and it must be a surprise. One cannot be too careful. You must pardon my inconveniencing you."

The man's words, softly spoken though precisely clipped in the manner of an accomplished linguist, were apologetic. Yet Eichelman, strangely, felt that all the consideration in them lay on the surface, that this lean, saturnine client of his was a creature without heart or human sympathy. For Eichelman was a judge of men as well as of jewels; and so he spread his hands deprecatingly.

"It is no trouble, your Highness," he said quickly. "I am dining in town tonight; the theater, perhaps, later. I close the shop; I relax—and then you are here."

The client smiled, and in his smile there was no softness.

"You have negotiated with me in complete secrecy, then, Eichelman?" he asked carefully. "It is necessary, for—"

Earnestly the jeweler replied, "The bill of sale will be kept in my personal safe. Only the insurance company will know."

The client seemed satisfied. "Four hundred thousand, I believe you said?" He readied into his breast pocket, withdrew a thin black checkbook.

Eichelman bobbed his head vehemently. "Four hundred thousand, yes, your Highness."

The other stared coldly at Eichelman. "My credit references were good?" he asked significantly.

Eichelman, suddenly choking, stammered respectfully, "Oh, yes, your Highness. Eminently satisfactory, I must say."

A bleak smile crossed that deeply chiseled face. Without a word the client wrote the check, shook it carefully with his left hand to dry the ink while with his right he restored Eichelman's patrician gold pen to its inkwell.

Avidly the jeweler watched. At last the check was sufficiently dry. The client, as if to tantalize the jeweler, leaned his elbows on the glossy desktop, held the check up between the thumbs and forefingers of both hands, directly beneath Eichelman's nose.

The jeweler, staring at the check as a baby might scrutinize some glittering bauble, was not immediately aware that the other's eyes, a scant three inches above the upper edge of the check and less than a foot from his own nose, had fixed themselves inflexibly upon his face.

Yet he felt uneasy.

His eyes lifted, met the gaze of that other, a gaze suddenly, incredibly smoldering, yet stone-like too, burning with the unearthly glare of scintillant rubies.

Uneasily Eichelman strove to turn his eyes aside, but could not. His attention had been caught, imprisoned by a will far stronger than his own. Suddenly he felt afraid, felt his mouth go dry and his nerves crumble. He wondered if he were unbelievably dreaming, wondered why he did not speak, yet made no attempt to open his lips. It was as though an enchantment, an hypnosis, had been thrown over him.

He waited, then, for the other to lower his eyes. But still that mind-shattering scrutiny burned into his skull. And then he realized that his brain was swirling, that a mist was forming across his vision. His client's face had suddenly grown dim; it danced and shimmered before him, lean, pallid, with thin red lips parted in a sardonic smile.

Eichelman, the strong-willed jeweler, knew that his senses were slipping from him like mist from the land, like fog from the water…

CHAPTER TWO
Silent Murder

SEAN O'SHAUGHNESSY, store detective in the employ of David Eichelman, jeweler, playing solitaire in the glass-enclosed bookkeeper's cage near and to the right of the bronze entry doors, was growing uneasy. When Mr. Eichelman had asked him to wait, tonight, he had tacitly admitted that he feared his mysterious client. Yet he had insisted on admitting the man himself, had kept O'Shaughnessy hidden!

It was twenty minutes of eleven. And for upward of two hours O'Shaughnessy's thoughts had strayed more and more from the cards toward speculation, speculation concerning what might be happening behind that closed door, back on the mezzanine floor.

Except for the faint slap of the cards and the sound of his own breathing the store was silent. No murmur of voices came through the thick plate-glass door of Eichelman's office, but this gave O'Shaughnessy no concern; he knew that the men within could be talking with reasonable loudness without the sound of their voices penetrating farther than the mezzanine. Only the sounds of altercation, of physical violence, would carry to where he waited, within a dozen feet of the entrance. And there had been no such sounds.

And yet O'Shaughnessy knew that something was wrong, hideously, quietly wrong. At last, as the minute hand of the clock approached eleven, knowing that he faced a severe reprimand from his employer for leaving the bookkeeper's cage without a more tangible motive, he could stand suspense no longer. Quietly, softly he threaded his way between the shrouded rows of showcases toward the stairs at the back of the store. Crouched just beyond the gleam of amber shining through the frosted glass into the mezzanine, he listened.

From within that closed door came only an unbroken, oppressive silence.

Grimly O'Shaughnessy knocked. There was no response. The silence within the room was tangible, like a living menace.

And then O'Shaughnessy tried the lock on the door. To his surprize, it yielded easily. O'Shaughnessy stepped quickly into the room, stopped short with a sudden, sibilant ejaculation.

David Eichelman sat at his kidney shaped, mahogany desk, facing the door, but the stranger had vanished!

And Sean O'Shaughnessy knew, instantly, that David Eichelman was dead, even though his eyes were half open, even though he slouched back easily in his chair, his right hand lying negligently on the desk before him. The immobility of his pose, the glaze on his eyes, the colorlessness of his face, told the detective that he was already dead.

O'Shaughnessy leaped toward the window that opened upon the court at the back of the building, peered into the blackness beyond the light from the office. Although it was pitch-dark out there he knew the topography of that courtyard—a blank-walled airshaft between adjoining buildings, a brick-lined chimney up which only a human fly could climb to freedom.

And, too, its importance only just beginning to register upon O'Shaughnessy's bewildered consciousness, loomed, inches before his eyes, the latticework of half-inch thick steel bars which protected Eichelman's back windows, bars so closely spaced that even the smallest child might not squeeze through!

Feeling a crawling begin at the base of his spine and sweep upward, shriveling the flesh like a needle spray as it passed, O'Shaughnessy gazed idiotically at those bars, at the dead jeweler, while waves of unreasoning, ghastly terror hammered through him. For, although the stranger had vanished, he had not left that room by the door and he could not have left it by the window…

With hands that had suddenly begun to tremble, O'Shaughnessy picked up Eichelman's French phone and dialed the police.

CHAPTER THREE
Strange Death

Police commissioner Charles B. Ethredge missed the first routine turmoil that followed O'Shaughnessy's call to headquarters for the sufficient reason that on this particular evening he had been entertaining at the theater and at supper the young lady he intended to marry. The first inkling he had of the case came as his car drew up softly before her apartment house.

The doorman, saluting respectfully, came hastily forward, extended the Commissioner a penciled note that had been left by a prowl car, anticipating his return to Mary's. Ethredge read the message, turned gravely to his fiancée.

"I must go, dear. A big case has just broken. Eichelman the jeweler's been murdered."

Like the thoroughbred that she was, she offered no objections, asked no questions. "I'm sorry, Charles boy. Call me in the morning, won't you, sweet?" She leaned toward him quickly and kissed his cheek. Then, before he could clasp her in his arms the car door had closed behind her. Just as she entered the foyer she turned, waved to him, smiled...

Slowly he meshed the gears. At first lingeringly, then gathering speed, the long black sedan moved into the city's traffic.

When Ethredge reached the jeweler's, most of the plain-clothes men, the photographers and the prowl-car boys had already left. But Lieutenant Peters of the Homicide Squad, three men from the Detective Bureau, a police physician, and an Assistant District Attorney were impatiently awaiting his arrival.

And in a corner of Eichelman's office rested a gruesome wicker basket, waiting to receive the body for its brief trip to the morgue.

The greetings were terse and matter of fact. Ethredge listened, for the most part without comment, to Lieutenant Peters' brief resume of the meager knowledge so far at hand. It wasn't much. It was made up half of O'Shaughnessy's story and half of the usual microscopic police that search for material clues.

"You are holding O'Shaughnessy for questioning?" Ethredge asked significantly.

Peters grinned and nodded. "His story sounded fishy to me. That stuff about Eichelman kotowing and scraping to some mysterious client he called 'Your Highness' struck me as made out of whole cloth."

Ethredge had been rummaging through the desk drawers. "I see that the treasurer of this firm is a fellow named Ben Sigal. Get him down here. We'll have to find out what's been stolen... No papers on Eichelman that might tell us anything about this mysterious nobleman of O'Shaughnessy's?"

"Eichelman's pockets had been rifled, Commissioner. Very leisurely and very carefully, I should say."

"Doesn't look so well for O'Shaughnessy," Ethredge commented briefly. Curiously he surveyed the corpse for the last time, preparatory to ordering its removal. "Say! He looks awfully pale! You'd think all the blood had been drained out of him! How the devil was he killed anyway, Hanlon? Make a guess; it doesn't cost anything."

Stiffly Doctor Hanlon answered, "We haven't undressed him, Commissioner. But I've examined him as well as I was able without disturbing him. I can say definitely that there are no major wounds, no traces of poison on the lips or in the mouth, no signs of asphyxiation. The unusual pallor you notice may be due to a form of anemia."

Ethredge laughed.

"In other words, Hanlon, you mean that you won't play. There isn't a mark on him bigger than a scratch; so you say that he hasn't any major wounds. Boy, but you're careful! Well, it looks to me as though he bled to death, with or without wounds."

The bantering tones faded from his voice.

"You'll do the autopsy in the morning. I'll want to know how he was killed, as soon as you've finished."

CHAPTER FOUR
A Transfusion of Blood

THE night had aged. The deep blackness that comes before dawn hung over the city like a sable pall; the city slept.

Yet Derwin, the attendant at the morgue, was not asleep. He had just received another body, and now, at the far end of the night, he was sitting in his little office, trying, with the aid of a detective magazine, to keep awake.

And so it was that he heard those sounds, those faintest of sounds, from that room at his back from which no sound should come!

Grumbling, his horse-face suddenly intent, he stood up, peered through the wire-reinforced square of glass set in the heavy oaken door.

The drama he witnessed robbed his body of strength, set his hands to trembling spasmodically, exploded his meager intelligence into instant insanity.

He saw the tall figure of a man moving from slab to slab, lifting the gray sheet momentarily from the face of each gruesome unfortunate, passing on. And at last he saw that tall figure whip the sheet from Eichelman's body and tumble it carelessly aside.

That tall figure, clad in formal evening clothes! He saw it sit on the edge of Eichelman's slab, bare Eichelman's arm to the elbow, perform the same strange operation upon its own.

From that moment Derwin, mouthing, trembling Derwin, could not have understood, even had he retained his sanity, the significance of what occurred. He could not have realized that the tall figure was giving the dead man a transfusion of its own blood!

And then, while his mouthings turned to inhuman screams, Derwin saw the body of Eichelman, the dead jeweler, stir and sit erect; he saw the lips of the dead man and his weird visitor moving in inexplicable conversation; he watched both men rise and go quickly to the barred window beyond the slabs, leap with inhuman agility to the sill, worm their way between bars so closely spaced that they would not admit the body of a full-grown cat, and disappear into the black night...

Slowly, slowly, as Derwin watched through dazed, mad eyes, the window closed...

And now no sound came from within that room of death. But from without the oaken door rose the hideous, unending cadence of a madman's screams.

CHAPTER FIVE
The Stolen Body

POLICE COMMISSIONER ETHREDGE, Lieutenant Peters and Mr. Benjamin Sigal sat in David Eichelman's office. It was close to dawn, and the three men were tired, their eyes red-rimmed. On the desk between them lay innumerable bundles of statements and packaged securities. The safe gaped open.

Ethredge addressed Sigal.

"Only the pearls are missing?"

"Only the pearls are missing, Commissioner."

Thoughtfully Ethredge rubbed a finger along his chin. "It would seem that Mr. Eichelman took them from the safe himself," he mused. "His fingerprints, alone, were on the dials."

"That strengthens O'Shaughnessy's story," Peters interjected.

Ethredge nodded. "Yes. Our criminal did not open the safe himself."

Abruptly he resumed his questioning of Sigal.

"Mr. Eichelman, you say, attended to all negotiations concerning these particular pearls?"

"Certainly. Mr. Eichelman personally conducted all the more important business."

"And so you don't know whether or not the list of possible buyers you have shown me is complete?"

"No. I do not."

"Have you heard Mr. Eichelman discuss the pearls with any prospective purchasers, either here in conference or on the telephone?"

Sigal, his brows wrinkling, went into a long resume of fragmentary conversations he had overheard, of the negotiations concerning which he had been informed, and of others which had seemed more secretive. Suddenly the Commissioner stopped him.

"You say," and Ethredge leaned forward eagerly, "that you overheard him discussing these pearls, on the telephone, with a customer to whom he spoke, deferentially, in both German and English?"

Sigal nodded.

"Find out," Ethredge said slowly, "what customers listed in your files have a knowledge of German. O'Shaughnessy says that when Eichelman let his mysterious stranger into the store last night the man spoke to him, using a decidedly guttural accent."

And Eichelman had addressed that stranger deferentially, as "Your Highness!"

"Find out, too," Ethredge continued, "what members of the nobility were among your customers!"

Suddenly, then, the telephone rang. Commissioner Ethredge forestalled Sigal, who had automatically reached toward the ivory and chromium mechanism, with a quick shake of his head. Picking up the phone, he put the receiver to his ear.

"Commissioner Ethredge speaking."

The voice coming over the wire sounded shatteringly loud in that tensely quiet room. Ethredge, as he listened, had to hold the receiver slightly away from his ear. But he heard the message to the end, put the receiver carefully in its cradle. And when he turned to Sigal and Peters his voice was harsh with amazement, amazement in which there was more than a hint of dread.

"That was the morgue," he said tersely. "Derwin, the night attendant down there, has gone stark raving mad. Eichelman's body has been—stolen!"

CHAPTER SIX
Perplexed

At exactly twelve o'clock noon on that, the second day of the Eichelman case, the buzzer on Commissioner Ethredge's desk at police headquarters sounded loudly. The Commissioner leaned forward swiftly and snapped a switch. The raucous voice of the switchboard operator filled the room. But Ethredge barely listened. Before he answered he had known that it would be Mary. Mary was always punctual.

He met her outside, in the grim stone corridor, clasped her small-gloved hands in a brief, wordless greeting. And then they were in the pleasant sunshine, away from that gloomy building which existed only for the punishment of human crime and folly.

"You're extra lovely today, Miss Mary Roberts," he told her, as she linked her arm in his and they stepped into the swirl of the noon-hour throng. She looked swiftly sideways at him.

"You haven't slept, Charles. Your eyes are tired."

He brushed his fingers carefully across his lean, whimsical chin. He had only had time for a shave and a quick shower on his way downtown from Eichelman's.

"You're eagle-eyed, Mary." They were passing a small restaurant. "Shall we go in here for lunch?"

As he ate, Charles told her of what had occurred during the night. And Mary, listening intently, was worriedly aware of the grayness that had overspread his face, the perplexity in his eyes, the hesitating uncertainty in his speech.

Gently, then, she said, "You shouldn't try to do everything yourself, Charles. The detective bureau is competent, and, after all, the sun doesn't rise and set in the Eichelman murder!"

"I'm not so sure," he said somberly. "Mary, if we take O'Shaughnessy's word as truth, the fellow becomes positively uncanny. And the snatching of Eichelman's body from the morgue! Who'd believe an incident like that? But it happened. And Derwin's in the City Hospital at this very moment, babbling about dead men walking, about a mysterious stranger in evening clothes coming through the window and engineering the escape of a corpse!"

Gloomily he paused, then went on.

"I was at the morgue myself, this morning. And those windows were—closed."

"But you said that the dust on one window sill had been disturbed," Mary reminded him. He stared at her.

"So it was," he admitted. "But, heavens, girl, no human being could have crawled through those bars, either at the morgue or at Eichelman's. It's an impossibility."

"That lets out O'Shaughnessy."

"Yes." For a few minutes he was silent, pondering. Then:

"The only clues—" he ticked them off on his fingers. "The man is tall; speaks with a German accent; wears evening clothes; was well enough known to Eichelman so that Eichelman would receive him alone after closing time in his own private office. He can go in and out of barred rooms as though the bars don't exist, and he kills without leaving any trace other than an appearance of bloodlessness in his victim." The worried lines across his forehead deepened.

They rose to go.

"Perhaps," Ethredge suggested, the old whimsical smile that she so loved returning, "you would check about among your society friends. Find out if any of our visiting counts, dukes, or barons seem to fit the specifications!"

CHAPTER SEVEN
A Corpse Returns

At eight-fifteen o'clock that evening Officer Baynes, on duty at Eichelman's, heard the brisk rapping of a gold-headed walking stick on the bronze door casing. Peering through the glass, he saw a small, roundly impressive man, seemingly in both an abominable humor and a great hurry to enter the store. Hesitating, the policeman saw the blows upon the door casing repeated with redoubled fury. Almost instantly the night bell buzzed angrily.

From within the store came the running footsteps of Mr. Benjamin Sigal...

"Dear God; it's Mr. Eichelman!"

The man's exclamation was a cry of sheer horror. His body sagged against the policeman's, the color drained from his face, leaving it yellow as old putty.

Officer Baynes felt a chill like the chill from a tomb sweep him. "Is it him as was *murdered?*" he whispered.

The blows on the door-casing were repeated with exceptional fury. "Open up, Sigal, you damned fool! What are you afraid of? Let me in, I tell you!"

With hands that trembled weakly, Officer Baynes opened the door. David Eichelman entered his own store.

"Don't stand there gaping at me like an idiot, Sigal! Come up with me to the office; I've had a hell of an experience."

For the first time he seemed to notice the officer. And in that instant his eyes blazed with red hate. "Well! They've got the police here watching the store, have they? That's just fine! And now," he stepped forward menacingly, "you get off my property!"

Bewilderedly Sigal protested, "But you were supposedly murdered. The police—"

Eichelman wheeled upon him like a cornered beast. "The police? Blunderers! Do I look dead?" He laughed, and there was something in that laughter that sent the flesh crawling.

"You cop! Get back where you came from!"

The policeman looked helplessly from the irate jeweler to Mr. Sigal.

"I've gotta stay here until I'm relieved." But then a sudden thought struck him. "I can report back that you're alive. That oughta end it. Lemme use the telephone."

Eichelman's face was thin-lipped, stony hard.

"You use no telephone in this store!" he snarled. "You get out of here. You go down the block and call your worthless police. I don't want to see hide nor hair of any of you again!"

Officer Baynes looked imploringly at Sigal. Sigal nodded reassuringly.

"Yes," he said, "better call from the drug-store at the corner. You may say that Mr. Eichelman is safe and that he doesn't want to see any policemen right now. Perhaps in an hour or so—"

"Not in an hour, either," Eichelman rasped. "Tomorrow, if at all. Now get out!"

The policeman retreated before the red wrath in Eichelman's eyes; for Eichelman was a property owner and a taxpayer. Eichelman could make life hard for him if he wished...

Alone with Sigal within the store, Eichelman led the way into his private office. They sat down. Mr. Eichelman did not speak. And as Sigal looked into his employer's eyes an uneasiness began to grow in him, to sweep upward within him until it dominated him, until it became *fear*. For, in some way, Mr. Eichelman had changed, subtly and horribly.

And then, suddenly, Mr. Eichelman stood erect, towered over his employee like an incredible doom. Sigal, looking fascinatedly into those red, red eyes burning down into his own, unable to tear his gaze away, felt mad terror clutch him, blanch his cheeks, stagger his nerve. And then Mr. Eichelman's fingers, strong as steel, were at Sigal's throat, were dragging Sigal, weakly struggling, across the desktop like a bundle of rags. For a brief instant Sigal saw his employer's face close to his own, saw the hellish triumph in his eyes, the cruel, inhuman sneer on his lips. Then merciful unconsciousness blackened the picture…

CHAPTER EIGHT
Another Victim

Although things had *looked* all right when he left Eichelman's, nevertheless Officer Baynes knew that he should have contacted Detective-Lieutenant Peters before leaving the premises. And so, within the drug store, he carefully refrained from mentioning the fact that he had left the jeweler's. He did say that Mr. Eichelman was in a towering rage.

Dismay swept him when Peters rasped out briskly, "That's neither here nor there about Eichelman. You stay where you are until you're relieved. I'll be right up!"

In a tumult of apprehension Baynes replaced the receiver and quickly made his way from the store. Had he been ten seconds earlier he would have seen Mr. Eichelman, carrying a briefcase, come hastily from the bronze portals of his own establishment and walk to a sleek, softly shimmering Rolls-Royce parked a few doors down the block. As it was, he only subconsciously noted the luxurious car, with its three occupants, as it purred past him, gliding with pantherine grace in the direction from which he had just come...

Arriving at the jeweler's, he tried the door, pressed the night bell. Utter silence answered.

Hardly before he had begun to realize the awkwardness of the position in which he had placed himself, a police car rolled up, disgorged Detective-Lieutenant Peters and two plainclothesmen.

"What's the matter here?" Peters exclaimed.

Stammeringly the poor devil replied, "Mr. Eichelman was boiling mad. Told me to get out and stand in the street."

Peters, for a moment, looked at the man. There was something impersonal, almost pitying, in that inspection. Then he said briefly, "I hope everything's all right in there. If it isn't this'll either cost you your badge or send you out pounding pavements in Yaphank Junction."

He jabbed vigorously at the night bell.

"Here, Baynes," he said after a moment, "get to a telephone and call this place; tell them to open up. You say Eichelman and Sigal are inside? Well, we've got right of entry here; this case isn't closed yet, by any means, even if Eichelman *is* alive. There's a jewel robbery on the books yet, don't forget that."

Twenty minutes later, to the accompaniment of a shattering of plate glass, the detectives entered the store.

They found Sigal in Eichelman's office, sprawled grotesquely across the desk, his terror-contorted face blotched with purple, yet white almost to ghastliness, his eyes wide open yet unseeing. With a startled oath Peters dropped to his knees beside the man. An exclamation of relief escaped his lips; for waveringly, faintly, Sigal's heart was still beating.

Roughly Peters forced whisky between Sigal's clenched jaws, drenched water across his face. And gradually Sigal showed signs of returning consciousness. He moaned feebly, his head rolled from side to side, his chest heaved. A detective, at the telephone, had already called an ambulance.

Suddenly, as Peters chafed Sigal's wrists, his eye caught an almost undetectable, reddish mark on Sigal's forearm. It was a puncture, directly over the radial vein, resembling the wound which might have been left by the recent use of a hypodermic needle.

Outside in the street sounded the brief wail of the ambulance siren. The white-coated ambulance crew entered;

without a word the intern dropped to his knees beside Sigal. After a brief moment he looked up.

"This man's in no immediate danger, but we'll take him down to the hospital and put him to bed. That choking," he pointed to Sigal's livid throat, "didn't do him any good. And he's damnably anemic."

But Peters, with a sudden sagging of his squarely hewn shoulders, had turned to the telephone, was dialing Commissioner Ethredge. For the safe door gaped open, empty jewel cases littered the floor, a flat steel securities box lay open on the tabouret, and a cyclonic litter of papers was strewn in utter confusion across the red and gold rug...

CHAPTER NINE
A Silver-bladed Dagger

AT four a.m. on the third calendar day of the Eichelman case Commissioner Ethredge and Detective-Lieutenant Peters prepared to leave, for the second successive time in as many nights, David Eichelman's store. Intensive hours of baffled investigation had left their nerves snapping and jangling, their bodies dog weary.

Two hundred thousand dollars in negotiable bonds and twice that value in gems had vanished in the second haul within twenty-four hours!

And at that moment, just as the men were about to lock that ravished office, a call came from headquarters.

David Eichelman's body had been found in a ditch on the Wolcott Beach Road—stabbed through the heart.

Ethredge swore one of his infrequent oaths. But behind that oath lay a renewed eagerness…

Within a few minutes the Commissioner's long black sedan was sliding smoothly through the suburbs, heading toward Wolcott. Ethredge drove in silence; Detective-Lieutenant Peters showed no inclination to talk.

There is no morgue at Wolcott. Ethredge drove directly to the red brick police station. Entering the building, they learned that Eichelman's body, for want of better facilities, had been placed on a couch in the small rest room just behind the sergeant's desk.

The Wolcott coroner was examining the body with a peculiar, strange interest.

Strange, because on the surface it looked obvious, sordid enough. A man lying dead in a ditch with a knife in his heart.

The body had been thrown from an automobile; there was no evidence that the murderer or murderers had even set foot to the road.

And yet the Wolcott coroner was studying that body with a painstaking intentness that seemed, somehow, almost fanatical.

He straightened, then, and shook hands with Ethredge and Peters.

"This man, Eichelman," he said puzzledly, "must have been thrown into that ditch sometime after dark last night, so that he'd been lying there a matter of ten hours, at the most, when he was found. Probably much less; he may have been dumped out only a few minutes before he was seen. But he was dead for a good many hours before his body was disposed of. Decomposition had quite definitely set in."

Commissioner Ethredge heard his own voice incredulously ask, "How long has this man been dead, Coroner?"

The Wolcott coroner was very positive. "Not less than thirty-six hours."

Musingly the Commissioner continued, "So that he must have been dead for at least twenty-four hours before he was dumped out in that ditch?"

The coroner nodded. "For at least twenty-four hours, yes!"

Ethredge and Peters looked at each other. They *knew* that Eichelman had been alive at eight o'clock last night! The statement the coroner had just made could not be true.

And yet—it was true. The coroner could not be mistaken.

His mind trying desperately to reconcile impossibilities, Ethredge picked up the dagger with which Eichelman had been stabbed, and held it gingerly by the tip of the blade. Something about it had attracted his attention.

"That's a funny-looking blade," he observed casually. "It doesn't look as though it came with the hilt. It looks homemade, as though it was cast in a mold, and then fastened into the hilt and sharpened afterward. Who'd want to do a thing like that?"

Suddenly, then, Peters, in a voice taut with a horror which he alone seemed to understand, gasped, "That blade isn't steel! It's something softer. Silver! It looks like silver to me!"

CHAPTER TEN
Count Woerz

The first brilliant rays of the sun were lancing above the horizon in a gigantic golden fan as Ethredge and Peters started back toward the city. Thoughtfully, his eyes alertly watching the road while his real consciousness studied the faint pattern of clues spread out within his mind, Ethredge muttered:

"God knows—we'll *have* to find, somehow, the explanation for these things that puzzle us now. And in the meantime we've picked up another bit of information. We've learned that our criminal drives an automobile."

"I suspect that he drives a Rolls," Peters interjected. "When I had Baynes on the griddle last night he managed to recollect seeing a Rolls pull away from Eichelman's, just as he was leaving that drug store."

"Check on that," Ethredge ordered grimly. "Or—wait. Better yet, I will let you off at the City Hospital. Sigal should be conscious by now. Ask him if any of Eichelman's customers own Rolls-Royces. I have a hunch that this fellow has traded at Eichelman's. He was acquainted with the jeweler, remember."

"You will be at headquarters?"

Suddenly Ethredge smiled. "I will be at headquarters within an hour. I am going to stop off and beg a breakfast from Mary. She might give me a lead, you know, along with my grapefruit and bacon."

Peters dropped off at the City Hospital. Ethredge drove home, bathed and shaved, put in a brief call to Mary, and continued on to her apartment.

Mary herself opened the door to his ring, ushered him into the breakfast room where already a percolator was bubbling cheerfully, bacon was grilling aromatically, grapefruit beckoned. She watched him, her dark eyes glowing, until he had finished and was sipping his coffee, black and unsweetened.

"What success, Charles?" she asked, then, quietly.

He shook his head wearily.

"And yet, Mary, you might rattle off that list of blooded acquaintances of yours who speak German. And who own Rolls-Royces!"

She closed her eyes, and her lips silently moved as she strove to recollect.

"Well, there's Bunny Brainard. He has a Rolls—but he's no nobleman, and he's girl-crazy. And there's Tony Casteloni; he's Italian, and he has some sort of title, but I don't think he speaks German fluently."

"We'll keep him in mind," Ethredge said, thoughtfully.

"And then there's Leopold—that's Count Woerz; he'd be just the man for you." Abruptly she paused, while a deep blush overspread her cheeks. Confusedly, then, she went on:

"He's sophisticated, you know; satanically handsome; wealthy; cosmopolitan; with a reputation as a heart-breaker. Serpentine, Charles; you loathe him and yet he fascinates you."

Her lashes lowered, her eyes darkened introspectively.

"I was quite intrigued by him myself, Charles, at one time."

"He must be the fellow we're after, then," Ethredge said, laughing.

But Mary resented that. "Don't jest, Charles. Count Woerz is really a fine gentleman. It's just that there's that strangeness about him. It's unfortunate, too. Recently there's been the silliest story going about that Katherine

Grant just pined away and died for love of him. If he hadn't looked like that—so—so sort of *devilish*—people wouldn't ever have thought anything of it."

"What *did* she die of, Mary?" Ethredge asked easily.

"Oh, it was some sort of anemia, I think. She had to have dozens and dozens of blood transfusions. But in the end she died. You can see for yourself how silly all that talk was…"

CHAPTER ELEVEN
The Count Has a Visitor

WAS Count Leopold Woerz the man? Five hours of intensive, painstaking labor had revealed an amazing series of facts. Commissioner Ethredge and Detective-Lieutenant Peters had definitely learned that Count Woerz *had* traded at Eichelman's—a diamond pendant, a few other small trinkets; they had learned that Count Woerz *did* own a Rolls-Royce, and they had learned that he was Eichelman's *only* noble client who ordinarily spoke German.

Were these facts mere coincidences, or were they a series of delicate clues, pointing unerring fingers toward an elusive criminal?

The additional bits of information the police had managed to secure concerning Count Woerz had not been encouraging. They had learned that he was no bogus nobleman, but that his title and right of entry into America were unquestionable; the Woerz family was one of the oldest and had been, before the war, one of the richest in Hungary. Count Woerz was, in a polite manner, a globetrotter. He was a man of considerable wealth.

Such was the character upon which Commissioner Ethredge had focused his attention.

Suddenly, with the startling unexpectedness of a dead man coming to violent life, he pitched his unlighted cigar into the wastebasket and stood up.

"I'm going out and pay a call on this Woerz gentleman, Peters," he announced.

Peters, without surprise, nodded. Ethredge strode almost light-heartedly from the room…

Count Woerz maintained his American residence in an ultra-expensive block of apartments; a twenty-ninth story Babylonian palace. Ethredge, debouching from the elevator, found himself in a richly inlaid, cathedral-ceilinged foyer. After a brief, appreciative glance about, he matter-of-factly rang a small bell suspended above a superb table upon which rested a shallow urn, obviously a repository for calling cards.

Presently the sound of footsteps came softly down a long corridor which extended back into the apartment, and Ethredge was confronted by a pudgy, blond man of indefinite age and oddly vacuous countenance. The footman did not speak, merely waited impassively.

"I would like to see Count Woerz," Ethredge said firmly. He extended his card. The footman took the card between the forefinger and thumb of his right hand and, without looking at it, dropped it in the urn on the table.

"Count Woerz is not at home. Count Woerz will be at home after eight," he said, in a colorless, guttural monotone.

The man was quite probably, Ethredge knew, both an old family servant and an idiot.

"I will return at eight-thirty," he said slowly, trying to make the man understand. The footman bowed stiffly, in a manner reminiscent of a mid-European foot soldier…

Ethredge left. But promptly at eight twenty-five he returned to that cathedral-like foyer, with its indirect lighting and its vaulted ceilings.

This time the bell was answered by a different manservant, presumably the butler, a rugged-looking, almost brutish individual, with cruel, thin lips and piercing eyes.

"Come with me, Commissioner," the man said shortly, as he took Ethredge's hat and stick. "Count Woerz has kept this time open for you, and has asked me to show you in to him immediately."

Was there a hint of contempt in his bruskness?

Turning abruptly, the man led the way down the long corridor and stopped at a small walnut door set inconspicuously in the superb paneling. Throwing open the door, he waited while Ethredge entered, then closed the door softly behind him.

The room in which Ethredge found himself was not large; it was a sort of den-library. The walls were lined up to the height of a tall man with bookshelves, crammed to capacity with volumes which Ethredge saw, even at a casual glance, were both costly and well read. A small desk stood near the center of the room, beneath a brilliant light suspended from the ceiling; at this desk sat a man. A comfortable armchair had been drawn up to within conversing distance of the desk.

The man rose, came out from behind the desk, extended his hand to Ethredge. And Ethredge, as they touched hands briefly, felt a shudder sweep him, exactly as he might react had he touched a snake or a frog. Struggling to control his revulsion he smiled, spoke briefly:

"Count Woerz?"

"Commissioner Ethredge. Please sit down."

Seated, facing the Count, Ethredge studied, without appearing to do so, this man he had so wanted to meet. At first glance he was disappointed; for the Count seemed merely a tall, sparsely built man, apparently thirty-five or so, a man with deeply lined features, smooth-shaven chin, hands of extraordinary length and delicacy, a receding hairline at the temples, which were slightly gray. He was conventionally dressed in a superb evening suit and snowy linen.

For a few minutes they made small talk. Ethredge in reality did not know what to say, and it was Count Woerz who gently, effortlessly, made conversation. But at last the Commissioner asked bluntly:

"Doubtless you wonder why I am here. Count Woerz."

The Count politely inclined his head. "I would be interested to know, yes. Although our conversation is pleasant, still—" He gestured toward the papers littering the desk.

Ethredge, as always when he felt a battle of wits impending, reached into his pocket and extracted his cigar-case. Opening the case, he extended it toward the Count. Woerz's lips curled in a swift, fragmentary smile.

"Thank you. I never smoke. But perhaps you would like some wine?" And he motioned toward a decanter standing at his elbow.

Ethredge hesitated. But the Count, smiling, poured two goblets of the wine. Lifting his own courteously to his lips, he gestured toward the other. Ethredge took up his glass.

"You knew Mr. David Eichelman?" he asked.

Count Woerz inclined his head. "From time to time I have purchased of him." He spoke casually, yet Ethredge felt convinced that he was alert as any crouching beast. The man's eyes had flamed dangerously.

"You know, then, that he has been murdered?" Ethredge persisted.

Count Woerz shrugged. "That is a matter of common knowledge. I am as well informed as the man in the street, I suppose."

Ethredge paused, for a moment, before he continued. He wanted the full significance of his next words to strike upon the Count without warning.

"You are aware that you have been identified as the mysterious visitor to the Eichelman store? Do you know that you were seen driving Mr. Eichelman from his own store in your car at approximately eight forty-five yesterday evening?"

A lurid glare blazed up, like a clangorous warning, in the Count's eyes, and then as quickly died away.

"You astonish me," he said quietly. "I might suggest that there has been some mistake."

Ethredge, certain as if by direct axiom that Woerz, incredible as it might seem, was the man, bluntly rasped, "There has been no mistake. You were involved in Eichelman's death!"

Foolhardy, to have let his nerves drag from him such a statement!

Count Woerz had leaned slightly forward in his chair.

"Then I am to consider myself under arrest?" he asked.

Commissioner Ethredge shook his head, cursing his own indiscretion.

"Not yet." He rose to go. Count Woerz was looking at him with a curious, gloating expression on his immobile, deeply chiseled face. His thin lips were startlingly blood red against the pallor of his face...

"Sit down!" The Count snarled the command.

Ethredge sank back watchfully into his chair. Woerz looked at him as one might study some insignificant insect that has suddenly developed a sting.

"A word of warning," the Count pursued significantly. "You are attentive to a Miss Mary Roberts?"

Ethredge let the impertinence pass without a reply.

The Count continued. "At one time she was not wholly indifferent to me. You will pardon me if I seem to speak with too much conceit, but I think that it would not be too difficult a task to win her away from you. That might be my revenge, should you continue to irritate me. As far as the Eichelman matter is concerned, you have made, in coming here tonight, a complete fool of yourself. Good evening to you, sir."

Commissioner Ethredge stood up angrily. Resisting an impulse to smash the man's lips into his too-pallid face, he turned to go. And then he caught a glimpse of the Count's goblet. It was still full to the brim; the wine had not been touched.

"You have not drunk your wine!" he exclaimed, astonished.

Count Woerz' lips smiled, and behind them Ethredge glimpsed cruel, pearly white teeth.

"I do not drink wine, Commissioner Ethredge. It reminds me of blood. You antagonize me, sir; I begin to think that I would sooner quaff a goblet of your blood than drink that wine! And now, please go."

Still with that mechanical, terrifyingly polite smile lingering on his face, Count Woerz watched the door close. Then, thoughtfully, he picked up the telephone and dialed Mary Roberts. "Mary?" he asked, when the maid had summoned her mistress to take the call. "This is Leopold…I would like to see you… Yes, it's urgent. Shall you be at Moore's bazaar this evening? …The dinner—I've wriggled out of that, but the gambling should be exciting. I'm to do the mind-reading, you know."

"I am not really…intimate with the Moores," Mary protested.

"But you're not doing anything in particular? Then come with me for the latter part of the evening. It should be an experience…"

CHAPTER TWELVE
"Like a Wolf!"

COMMISSIONER ETHREDGE, back at police headquarters, sat down at his desk and rested his forehead in his hands. Dear God, what a mess! Not one speck of evidence against Woerz. Baynes wasn't even certain that the car he had seen had been a Rolls. O'Shaughnessy hadn't glimpsed the face of the man Eichelman had admitted to the store. Not one incriminating fingerprint had been found.

And the papers were clamoring for an arrest...

Too, that stubborn coroner at Wolcott had reported Eichelman's body brimming with fresh blood, while twenty-four hours earlier Doctor Hanlon had been as emphatic in the opinion that Eichelman had just undergone a transfusion drastic enough to deplete his veins to the point of anemic death!

How could the body of a man forty hours dead and already in the first stages of decomposition contain an oversupply of living blood?

Feeling that to sit idly there much longer would drive him half-mad, Ethredge leaped to his feet, took two swift strides, flung open the door.

"Peters!"

From the doorway of a room down the corridor Peters' head protruded.

"Come in here and keep me company," Commissioner Ethredge ordered, "before I go crazy."

Within his office he told Peters all that had occurred, every word that had passed between Woerz and himself.

"The man's foul," he said earnestly. "I can feel the evil in him just as I'd feel it, looking at a rattlesnake. He's like a wolf."

Almost as though speaking to himself Peters murmured, "Like a *wolf*, Commissioner? I wonder!"

There was a hint of earnestness in the strange remark that startled Ethredge. "What do you mean?" he asked slowly.

But Peters evaded the question. "I'd rather not say any more now, Commissioner. You'd think me insane. But I'd like to see that fellow myself, sometime."

"You'll see him," the Commissioner promised grimly... There was silence between them.

Suddenly Ethredge spread his hands helplessly. "Damn it, Peters; I'm fidgety. I think that I'll go over to Mary's and cadge a drink."

He picked up the telephone. And Mary's maid, answering, told him that "Miss Mary has gone to the Moores'—to the bazaar. Count Woerz called for her."

Stunned, Ethredge put down the telephone. He looked across the desk at Peters.

"Are your evening clothes pressed, Peters?" he asked, with seeming irrelevance. His voice was strained, unnatural.

"I guess so," Peters assented. "They were pressed fresh for the Saint Patrick's Day ball."

Ethredge wet his dry lips with his tongue. "Well, go home and put them on. We're going to drive out to Mrs. Weston B. Moore's bazaar. And perhaps if we're fortunate you'll see Count Woerz, face to face!"

CHAPTER THIRTEEN
Mrs. Moore's Bazaar

Mr. Weston B. Moore was one of the many who had been mushroomed to richness by the Coolidge boom and one of the few who had retained his estate after the crash. A general opinion in more conservative circles was that Mr. Moore had never been overly honest…

Be that as it may, whenever Mrs. Weston B. Moore did anything she did it grandly. Her bazaar was no exception to this rule. She had dotted her gardens with thousands of multicolored lanterns. A floor had been put down on one of the terraces where dancing went on, to the purr of a thousand-dollar orchestra. Scattered at a dozen strategic points along the walks and paths a corps of white-coated waiters mixed drinks for the ever-moving throng. A score of brightly colored booths, presided over by members of Mrs. Moore's own particular set, were variously billed: *Your Fortune Told—A Night in the Orient—Kisses*. Gambling, at cards and by machine, went on in half a dozen rooms within the house. A troupe of Javanese dancing girls entertained at hourly intervals on the lawn.

Over all this scene of extravagance and semi-drunkenness presided, reluctantly, it must be said, the Spirit of Charity.

Mrs. Moore herself, a somewhat fleshy, artificial blond, welcomed Count Woerz and Mary at her little table set strategically at the entrance to the grounds. She greeted Woerz effusively; toward Mary she was gushingly polite.

"I *knew* that you'd arrive at just this time!" she chattered. "I was telling all the guests at dinner how you abhor dining out. All those who haven't already met you are just dying to meet a man with such an ecentricity! And when I told them that you were going to tell the fortunes!"

"Not tell the fortunes," Count Woerz corrected, smiling. "Just mind-reading, you know, it's merely trickery."

"Oh, but I'm sure there's much more to it than an *act*, Count Woerz! That sounds so sordidly professional. I've told everyone how you've been in Tibet, and China, and all those supernatural countries. You'll be quite the rage. You've always seemed so thrillingly mysterious!"

Count Woerz frowned. "I have never tried to appear mysterious," he said quickly. "I have always tried to seem as—as normal and human as possible."

Mrs. Moore blushed. "You're so modest! But now, I'm keeping you from the bazaar with all this prattle. I'm so sorry. Do anything you want to amuse yourselves, my dears, and so glad to see you here, Miss Roberts. And at what time would you like to take a booth for the mind-reading, Count Woerz?"

The Count hesitated. "Well, not too late. Say from— from eleven until twelve. That would give your professional person an hour's relaxation."

Mrs. Moore gurgled ecstatically. "Splendid! I'll have the arrangements made right away. And don't make your—your sittings, or whatever they're called, too long. Just tell each person something startling about himself and then go on to the next. I've built you up into a sensation, Count Woerz. We're charging fifty dollars a sitting for your demonstrations."

Unaccountably, Count Woerz seemed displeased…

AS MARY ROBERTS and Woerz strolled slowly about the grounds, stopping here and there to try their luck at the games of chance or to purchase some absurdly over-priced knicknack, they passed the gypsy tent. And this, unlike the greater part of Mrs. Moore's bazaar, was genuine. The tent was old and battered; the banner, once gaudy and bright, showed a thousand patches and seams. And the ballyhoo was called out by a hook-nosed, swarthy man with the restless, black eyes of a true gypsy. Two children, squatting timidly on the ground beside the tent, were obviously the offspring of the fortune-teller, Romany wife of the gypsy. Wherever Mrs. Moore had picked up her fortune teller, and presumably she had engaged the woman through some theatrical agent, she had secured a touch of authenticity which most of her show sadly lacked.

And then a strange incident occurred. Mary had stopped, fascinated, to watch the gypsy children. The man had for the moment discontinued the ballyhoo; for a client had just entered the tent. Count Woerz lounged a few feet away.

The gypsy glanced casually at the Count. The eyes of the two men met.

Perhaps some thought had been in the Count's mind, some thought which had left him temporarily oblivious of his surroundings.

The gypsy, gazing into those blankly staring eyes, suddenly shuddered, shrank into himself, seemed to shrivel with terror. And then, with trembling hand, he made the sign of the Cross!

Abruptly, then, Count Woerz did a strange thing. He grasped Mary's arm roughly, led her away…

"You'll miss the Javanese dancing girls," he explained, when she protested…

Following the line of booths, they reached the end of the midway. And presently the Javanese girls danced. Mary watched this portion of the entertainment with genuine pleasure; the Count, however, stood beside her with that air of semi-detachment with which he seemed to survey all human activity, as though it surrounded him without affecting him in the least.

As they were returning, Count Woerz looked at his watch.

"Will you dance, Mary, while I'm—entertaining? Or would you prefer to gamble?"

She considered. "I'd rather not dance. So many of the people here are strangers. But I wouldn't mind a whirl at the numbers."

He stopped at the entrance to the house, took a thin sheaf of crisp new bills from his pocket and gave them to her.

"If you win, we share equally. If you lose, the money is lost. What is money?"

CHAPTER FOURTEEN
A Second Too Late

Commissioner Ethredge and Detective-Lieutenant Peters reached the Moore's bazaar just as the announcement was being blared through amplifiers suspended above the midway, that Count Leopold Woerz was now in the tent of the Past, the Present, and the Future, and that for one hour he would demonstrate the art of mind-reading.

Oddly, Mrs. Moore had commandeered the gypsy tent.

"You wanted to meet Woerz," Commissioner Ethredge said somberly. "Here is some money. I had expected to donate something anyway; it's better invested this way."

About a hundred persons had gathered before the faded tent. Several in the front rank seemed on the verge of paying their money and finding out for themselves what truth there was in Mrs. Moore's extravagant statements.

The first client, a middle-aged, portly gentleman, had passed through the loose canvas flap into the tent. And apparently Count Woerz, for the benefit of charity, intended to separate these people from their money with the greatest possible dispatch; for in not more than a minute and a half the client popped out again, a slightly dazed expression on his face, muttering incoherently to himself.

Woerz's first success had aroused the interest of the crowd, so that the line had become of respectable length. Commissioner Ethredge felt relief when he saw that Peters had managed to gain a place among the first half-dozen; at that rate he would be inside the tent within ten minutes.

Woerz mowed them down with machine-like regularity. They were only in the tent for a moment; then they came stumbling out, with dazed, half-silly expressions on their faces.

The man must, Commissioner Ethredge mused, be genuinely adept.

And Detective-Lieutenant Peters, now almost at the head of the line, had realized the gravity of the position in which he had placed himself; had determined to keep his mind fixed upon some inane jingle. Particularly, no thought of his should reveal his identity or his profession to the Count.

As he was making this decision he found himself at the head of the line; in the next instant he felt the fifty-dollar fee being taken from his hand, realized that he was passing through the dirty canvas flap into the tent.

Within the tent a single electric light burned overhead; two gilt chairs, a table on which rested the gypsy's professional tools—a crystal ball and a pack of greasy playing cards—were the total furnishings.

But it was only subconsciously that Peters took notice of these things; his whole attention was riveted on the man sitting bolt upright in the chair before him. Tall, almost emaciated, with aquiline chin and nostrils, the man stared at him through piercing, glowing eyes. For the rest, Count Woerz's face was impassive as the face of a dead man. His cheeks were deathly white. Only the thin line of his lips was brilliantly red, as though artificially carmined.

These impressions flashed through Peters' brain in the span of a second. Feeling something unaccountably like panic welling up in him, he set his mind to repeating, over and over:

"The clouds up in the sky so high; the clouds up in the sky so high."

Count Woerz's thin lips moved.

"Sit down," he said. Then, immediately, "The clouds up in the sky so high'; you're resisting. It doesn't matter to me; if you resist you only waste your own money. What's your name?"

Peters' lips were silent, but automatically his mind had answered. The Count smiled.

"Peters. Your occupation? Police officer?" A cold light had flared in his eyes. "That's interesting. Do you know Police Commissioner Ethredge? Do you know me? And you think of me in connection with David Eichelman?"

The Count leaned forward earnestly. "You realize how impossible it is to connect me with Eichelman— how absurd it is. Don't annoy me further, please…"

And then, suddenly as the rush of an electric current along a wire, Peters' brain reverted to its original purpose. And as he thought, simultaneously Count Woerz read his thought, for as Peters' hand plunged into his own breast pocket the nobleman's body catapulted forward, struck the gleaming rectangle from Peters' hand to the dirt-stained matting. And then Count Woerz's gleaming shoe had crushed down upon it, shattering it into a hundred fragments…

Frantically Peters strove to recall that inane sentence to his mind:

"The clouds up in the sky so high; the clouds up in the sky so high…

Venomously Count Woerz spoke.

"You have some very peculiar suspicions, Mr. Detective-Lieutenant Peters. I advise you to put them from your thoughts. They belong to the Middle Ages, to Medieval Europe, not to modern America. Should you dare to express them you would be laughed out of countenance. Now go."

He did not know that in striking the mirror from Peters' hand, he had been a second too late. But Peters' mind was reeling with what he had seen!

CHAPTER FIFTEEN
Mary Roberts

Peters' face, as he reeled from the gypsy tent, was the color of chalk. His lips were moving as though he was speaking to himself; stark horror gleamed in his eyes.

A pleased gasp went up from the onlookers; Count Woerz was proving a sensation...

Hurriedly Commissioner Ethredge stepped forward, grasped Peters' elbow and led him away from the crowd. Peters was staggering drunkenly. Ethredge, selecting a deserted spot behind a clump of trees, paused. Peters had not uttered a word.

And then Peters put his hand before his face, retched, and was violently sick!

"In God's name," Ethredge asked hoarsely, "what happened in there?"

Peters shook his head. His face was bedeviled with perspiration.

"I can't—tell you now, Commissioner. It's—it's beyond belief. Wait—wait until we get where we can talk. Get—get me a drink, please."

Ethredge returned quickly to the midway, found one of the refreshment booths.

"A tumblerful of rye," he ordered bruskly.

The white-coated attendant's eyebrows flickered, but he filled the order. Ethredge took the drink, put down a ten-dollar bill and turned back down the midway.

As he passed the gypsy tent he suddenly paused. A man had just come from that tent, a man darkly suave, with a livid scar on his left cheek that might have been made, twenty or more years before, by the slash of a saber.

Commissioner Ethredge felt the uncomfortable certainty that he should know this man...

Peters, almost without pause, gulped the whisky Ethredge had brought. It seemed to steady him; with the support of Ethredge's arm he was able to walk back to the midway.

And then Ethredge saw, standing at the entrance to the grounds, Count Woerz and Mary! They were just about to enter Count Woerz's Rolls Royce. Ethredge grasped Peter's arm.

"Come, Peters; get hold of yourself. We've got to follow them!"

The brutal-looking, animalesque man who had, earlier in the evening, admitted Ethredge to Count Woerz's apartment was now, in chauffeur's livery, closing the door of the car, climbing into the driver's seat. Slowly, then gathering speed, the car slid away into the darkness.

CHAPTER SIXTEEN
Hypnosis

As the car rushed softly through the night Count Woerz spoke solicitously to Mary.

"Tired?" he asked. There was a world of kindliness in his voice. He looked at her speculatively, was secretly pleased. For she was sitting relaxed, with her right cheek turned to catch the caress of the night air; there was no tenseness in her, no watchfulness.

"No, not tired." She fumbled in her handbag, drew out a roll of bills which she handed to him. "I lost," she mourned.

He took the money, put it away without counting it. "No matter. I expected you to lose. Did you enjoy playing?"

She laughed briefly. "As well as anyone could under the circumstances, I suppose."

"Then the money is well spent," he assured her.

Presently he spoke again, a little sadly, Mary thought: "Look at me, Mary. You are not afraid of me?"

Their eyes met: the Count's faintly luminous, glowing with gentleness; Mary's warm with the friendship she was trying to give this lonely, misunderstood man. And in her heart was the thought, "People have been cruel to him. They've the— the unconscious feeling that he's a sort of monster. But—he isn't."

"I am not afraid of you," she breathed.

"Look at me," he whispered.

His voice was like the restful music of a muted hymn. Listening to him speak, she felt a delicious urge to relax, to let her eyelids droop softly shut. She felt apart from herself, drifting in a dream world of utter unreality. The night-bound landscape hurrying by, the drone of the motor, the twin-eyed cars that rushed past in frequent crescendos of sound and light, had dwindled from concrete reality to the incorporeality of shadows. The only reality left had merged within Count Woerz's eyes: she felt that if only she could look into them deeply enough she could read there all the unanswerable enigmas of the ages. They glowed like the eyes of a god…

Dimly, deliciously, she felt herself sliding, with ever-increasing velocity, down the sides of an infinite vortex. Count Woerz's eyes were expanding, growing into twin suns, lurid, fateful, blood-tinged. The incline down which she seemed to be tobogganing became an almost vertical precipice.

Hot, nerve-torturing fear engulfed her. Desperately she tried to struggle back upward along that incredible slope toward consciousness. But now the precipice had vanished utterly. She was falling, falling, falling with ever-increasing velocity into nothingness.

And then Count Woerz's eyes seemed to expand until they filled her whole universe, seemed to explode in a final blaze of malignant light! And after that—darkness…

Count Woerz abruptly sat erect, looked down at the girl sitting, staring with wide-open, blind eyes into the utter blackness of complete hypnosis. The gentleness had vanished from his eyes; they burned in the semi-darkness with feral intensity. He spoke to her.

"You are hypnotized," he said slowly. "I am your master. You will succumb to me whenever I call, wherever you are. Do you understand?"

"I understand," Mary said. No vestige of controlling intelligence touched the words she uttered with personality and life.

The Count bent forward, brushed his hand several times before her eyes, spoke to her. With startling suddenness she awoke.

"Did I—did I faint?" she asked, bewildered. "For a moment I felt terribly dizzy."

"You were—a trifle pale," he reassured her. "It must have been the smoke in the roulette room…"

CHAPTER SEVENTEEN
A Naked Skull

COMMISSIONER ETHREDGE and Detective-Lieutenant Peters had doggedly followed the Rolls-Royce into town. Incredulously, now, they were watching Count Woerz matter-of-factly escort Mary to her door.

Count Woerz had recrossed the sidewalk, was re-entering his car. Silently the two men watched the Rolls-Royce pull away from the curb, merge into the city's traffic.

Urgently, then, Peters spoke. "Commissioner, we've got to go somewhere where we can talk. That—that *thing* is dangerous. We've got to make plans."

Unsurprised, Ethredge assented. "Come to my home, Peters. I mix a pretty decent highball…"

And Ethredge did mix a pretty decent highball. Yet Peters, sitting in one of the Commissioner's comfortable chairs, the tall drink within easy reach of his hand, found it difficult to begin.

"Commissioner," he said at last, "have you ever read about vampires?" There! He had broached the subject.

Ethredge fiddled with his glass. "Oh, a bit at the library," he admitted. "And I've seen a few melodramatic pictures."

"Commissioner," Peters said earnestly, "vampires do exist. And Count Woerz is a vampire."

Ethredge laughed. "Nonsense, Peters. Vampires belong in the same category with ghosts and witches and all the other superstitions of the Middle Ages. You don't feel—you don't feel sick, or anything?"

Peters shook his head. "I feel all right." He picked up his drink, took a meager sip, set down the glass.

"Commissioner," he went on, with that strange earnestness, "the world has believed in vampires for thousands of years. In every country, among every race, among both the most intelligent and the most ignorant we find a strongly ingrained belief in vampirism. An unfounded superstition could never have taken root like that, could never have surmounted the barriers of language, could never have crossed oceans and deserts, enduring through centuries."

Ethredge moved restlessly. "Folklore," he muttered.

Peters nodded. "Folklore, certainly, but folklore in which sixty percent of the world's peoples believe, today; folklore which always springs, if we search deeply enough, from an easily identifiable, unchangeable similarity of phenomena. The attributes of the vampire are the same, Commissioner, whether you hear of him in America or whether you hear of him in Burma. He's demonstrated his existence for ages, Commissioner. What we've failed to do is to study him and find out what he really is."

"The undead," Ethredge nodded. "Not dead; not alive. Well, I'll listen. But I warn you that I won't be convinced."

A deep, expectant silence rested, for a moment, over the room. And then, at first almost diffidently, Peters began to speak.

"I've read about these things," Peters said, as if apologetically, "not so much because of any belief in them, but because I wondered how the legends of vampirism could have become so widespread. I wanted to find out why whole races of people could have deluded themselves with tales so impossible. My main reaction, at first, was a sort of wonder that the stories of vampirism I read should all possess such fundamental similarities. I could not find any satisfactory reason why this should be so.

"But gradually and unwillingly I was forced to accept the view that the legends of vampirism are based on fact, however obscured by the imagination and the ignorance of the narrators. And at once my interest in this whole train of desultory study became intense. I set out to sift the truth from fiction, to determine, if possible, what fundamental characteristics of vampires are worldwide and subject to scientific scrutiny. I wanted to learn just what a vampire could or could not do, to attempt to reconcile him with natural laws; in short, to explode the whole legendry of vampirism. Already, from the fundamental similarities I had found to be characteristic of every vampire, I had begun to favor the idea that so-called vampires might really be members of some rare cult, very possibly possessing considerable powers of hypnotism, very possibly stronger, physically, than most men, due, perhaps, to extremely rigorous diet and exercise. The almost universal legend that vampires live solely on human blood seemed to uphold this hypothesis."

Commissioner Ethredge seemed relieved. "I've no objection to what you've said, so far," he admitted.

PETERS dourly shook his head. "I will tell you more… I discarded, of course, as many of the impossible attributes with which vampires have been empowered as I could. I disbelieved that they could change their shape; that they could appear as wolves or bats, for example. However, favoring my theory of vampirism as a cult, I admitted that by hypnotism they could produce just such illusions. And I saw no reason why the vampire could not cross running water, or why garlic should be offensive to him. I traced the belief in the efficacy of the cross against him to the Church, which in medieval times recommended the cross and the use of holy water against all powers of evil. I believed that the vampire could be killed by a stake driven through his heart, and I believed that he could be killed by a silver bullet or dagger, but I also surmised that a lead bullet or a steel knife would do the business just as well. Oddly, in all my research I found few authenticated, so to speak, accounts of vampire destruction.

"I utterly disbelieved that a vampire could be a man who had died and was now 'undead', the term by which vampires are designated. I was certain that he would cast a reflection in a mirror."

He paused, shuddered convulsively.

"Count Woerz—cast a reflection," he whispered, then. "I took a mirror into that tent, looked into it—looked at Count Woerz in it. Yes—he cast a reflection."

With difficulty he went on. "That is about where I was, a dilettante in the study of vampirism, when the Eichelman case broke. And now, Commissioner, I've had to adjust myself to reality, to explain to myself a form of unholy life which should never live, and yet does live! For, Commissioner, Count Woerz is a vampire, and he is almost as the old legends have described him!"

"You mean that he is dead and yet alive?" Ethredge asked slowly. "Nonsense!"

Peters shook his head. "I don't know. Science will explain him, must explain him. I don't know if he has ever really died, or if in some gruesome way the advent of death has been suspended.

"He cast the reflection of a skull, Commissioner—of a naked skull, with living red blood coursing over it and through a mass of gray putrefaction! By what rare natural law that thing presented to us the appearance of a man I do not know; there is powerful hypnotism in it. Woerz is a *thing* that should have been dead twice ten years ago; he is a skeleton sheathed in living pus and rich red blood. That explains how he forced himself between the bars at the morgue; there was only the lank skeleton of him and a mass of slime to pass through that narrow space."

"Eichelman, though, was but recently dead," Ethredge pointed out.

"I took a mirror into the tent, and looked at Count Woerz in it."

Peters nodded. "Woerz had sucked his blood, had infected him. Eichelman, too, was a vampire. Putrefaction was in him; putrefaction began in him even before O'Shaughnessy found his body. Remember the coroner at Wolcott saying that he must have been dead thirty-six hours, when we knew that he was seen alive the preceding evening?"

Gravely, then, Peters nodded his head. "Vampires are, indeed, dead-alive. They are creatures in which, by some rare process, the body which should be in the grave yet moves and, horribly changed, lives!"

He was silent. And they noticed, then, that the first gray light of dawn was striking into the room, dimming, making ghostly the warm glow of the lamps.

Ethredge laughed feebly. "Your vampire sleeps now," he said. "It is day."

Peters caught his breath. Might Ethredge be right? Might he, all along, have acted the fool, have sought too determinedly to disbelieve those things he had read of vampires? Might it not be that, almost in their entirety, the legends were right? Perhaps vampires *did* sleep from dawn to sunset. Could it not be plausible that the non-human processes which controlled their existence were affected by the clean sunlight?

Too, might not the silver bullet harm the vampire where steel and lead would not? Was his unhuman physiological structure antipathetical to silver? And to garlic?

These thoughts swept Peters.

"Commissioner," he said, "it is possible that you are right, that Woerz is asleep. We have no time to lose. We will go to his house and destroy him!"

CHAPTER EIGHTEEN
A Desperate Resolve

Half the day had passed, yet Ethredge and Peters had made no move toward Woerz's destruction. Instead, they were within the Commissioner's prosaically business-like office, arguing, arguing, arguing behind locked doors.

The homely routine of bathing, of changing into clean linen and breakfasting, had influenced Ethredge in a manner Peters should have foreseen. As the events of the night had receded into the sharp reality of day he had begun to disbelieve those things which so few short hours ago had seemed plausible.

"The man's unquestionably a murderer, Peters," Ethredge was saying vehemently. "But we can't walk into his house and deliberately execute him on the grounds of any such wild hypothesis as yours. The law must take its natural course."

Peters cursed. "But, man, you don't know what hell you're letting escape! Can't you see that today, before sundown, is our last chance? Tomorrow he'll be gone. But last night he didn't have time to—to break up that unholy lair of his. He's there, now."

With the abruptness, then, of one coming to a sudden decision, Ethredge snapped, "I'll tell you what I'll do. I'll gamble my career, and yours, too, against Woerz. We'll arrest him, search his apartment. But if we find no incriminating evidence against him—"

Peters, grimly satisfied, nodded.

CHAPTER NINETEEN
The Undead

"Gone!" It had taken an hour's work with crowbar and ax to force the steel door leading from the elevators into Woerz's foyer.

"Gone!" Peters whispered, again.

That whole vast apartment remained deathly silent, still as the nave of a cathedral at midnight…

The two men entered the corridor, stalked along its length, their feet sinking without sound into the rich pile of the rug. As they proceeded they tried the various doors. Some opened easily, revealing rooms of garish luxury. A few were locked.

They had come, seemingly, to a palace deserted and abandoned by its occupants, waiting only for the life and laughter of some new master to make it a place of ethereal beauty.

"The den!" Ethredge rasped grimly.

Crowbar and ax sent the inch-thick walnut panels splintering inward. The room flooded into light. Peters had turned on the desk lamp.

But a search of Count Woerz's desk proved fruitless. Not an incriminating paper, not an ambiguous document.

From the desk Ethredge and Peters proceeded to the bookcases, took down book after book, ruffled the pages hopefully. Not satisfied, they sounded the walls, searched under the rugs and behind the pictures. And the search revealed—nothing.

At last Ethredge, standing in the center of the room, grunted, "We can't waste more time here, Peters. But we've already put our necks in the noose. Might as well search those other locked rooms."

And, just within the ax-shattered door of that next room, Ethredge and Peters stopped short in astonishment.

It was gloomy within that room, almost dark. Opaque curtains covered the windows; the only light that entered came from the corridor. And yet there was enough light for both men to see that the room was a richly furnished bedchamber.

On the silken coverlet of the bed lay a woman, beautifully gowned, her hands lightly crossed above her round young breasts, her hair in immaculate perfection, her lips slightly parted, revealing the gleam of dazzlingly white teeth. The heels of her silver slippers rested daintily on a pad of velvet carefully spread upon the coverlet.

"God!" Ethredge breathed, as he stepped into the room. "She must either be dead or she must sleep soundly!"

He moved swiftly to the bed, took the girl's wrist lightly between his fingers, stood in silent concentration. Then, shaking his head, he bent down, slipped the smoothly shimmering evening gown down off the girl's satiny shoulders, placed his ear against her softly molded breast. "She's—dead!"

Peters had turned on the boudoir lamp, and was beside him, staring down at the body. Idly he picked up an arm, let it fall back limply. And it seemed to him that although the flesh was cold it was not the cold of clean, human death. Rather it was the cold of unnamable horror, of something that invoked revulsion, of uncleanliness—of uncleanliness in beauty.

"Not dead," he croaked, "but undead. See—the red in her lips, the smile on her cheeks. A corpse lies flat, sags down like a bundle of rags. But she looks as though she might open her eyes and speak to us."

"Catalepsy," Ethredge muttered. "We must get a doctor. She's too young to die—and too beautiful."

Peters' eyes were hard. "Not catalepsy. Get a mirror!" He turned, looked about the room. And then he gasped.

There was not a mirror in all that place of luxury!

"Commissioner," he said slowly, then, "will you believe me if I show you proof?"

Gravely, Ethredge nodded.

"Then ring for the elevator. Go out and get a mirror. Bring it back here." He sat down on the edge of the bed without a glance at the statuesque beauty lying, evening dress disheveled, so close beside him.

The sound of Ethredge's footsteps receded from the room...

Peters' eyes returned, fascinated, to the girl's face.

"I wonder who she—was?" he asked himself somberly. He studied her face more intently, and the sheer beauty of her almost took his breath away. Yet it made him uneasy, too; for it was a beauty that he had never seen in any woman in life, a wanton, soulless beauty. And gradually, as Peters became more uneasy, he felt the flesh on his scalp tightening...

And then Ethredge came quietly into the room, crossed over to the bed, stared down at the recumbent figure. He carried a small leather packet; he had had to go, Peters guessed, to a corner drug store and purchase a combination toilet set to get the mirror. There was a puzzled, intent expression on Ethredge's face.

"Turn on that ceiling light, Peters. I've—I've an idea I've seen this woman before."

Silently Peters watched the Commissioner, beneath the now brilliant illumination, studying that still, beautiful face.

"I know that I've seen her," Ethredge muttered. "But where? She greatly resembles Katharine Grant; only

Katharine never had a sister. And of course," he mused, "Katharine's dead."

Abruptly he paused. He had recalled Mary's words, "Recently there's been the silliest story going about that Katharine Grant just pined away and died for love of him."

"Go ahead, Peters," he said, then. "Go ahead with your mirror experiment!"

WITH hands that trembled Peters opened the leather case and extracted a cheap, rectangular mirror. Carefully he placed himself so that the light falling upon the still, siren's face would be reflected at its greatest intensity…

He looked into the mirror. For a moment the expression on his face did not change, but remained taut with anticipatory revulsion, tense as though he steeled himself against a sight of horror, Surprisingly, then, the sickening dread passed somewhat from his eyes, although his hands still trembled violently. With an odd gesture of finality he passed the mirror to the Commissioner.

"It is not so—horrible as the other," he muttered. "Thank God! How long has the Grant girl been dead?"

"Six—seven months," Ethredge replied.

Peters put a hand on his arm. "Woerz had been dead for twenty years," he mumbled. "It is she. Look for yourself."

As Ethredge looked into that mirror, great beads of perspiration stood upon his forehead, the color drained from his face; for, seen in reflection, that face that should have bloomed with petal-like freshness was mottled with great grayish spots, blotched with angry purple. And over the whole face was spread a tinge of saffron, deepening in places almost to the dead brown of dried leaves.

"A face of death," Ethredge whispered. "Of death, preserved from decay by the embalmer's art."

He had dropped the mirror and was staring incredulously at that still face; for once more it was the pallid, faintly tinted face of a sleeping girl!

"Peters!" he asked hoarsely, then, and his voice shook, "what ghastly magic is in that mirror? What law is behind all this?" And, as a macabre thought struck him, "I wonder if this woman would photograph—as she looks in that mirror!"

Doggedly, then, he stood up, his face stern, his body tense.

"Will she remain asleep?" Apprehensively he glanced at the recumbent girl.

"The legends say—until sundown," Peters answered, with horrible conviction.

"Then come. We'll search those other rooms—for Count Woerz!"

CHAPTER TWENTY
In the Vampire's Power

The first room Ethredge and Peters searched, exquisitely furnished, was obviously a guest room. And, surprisingly, it contained a mirror, a superb affair set in a heavy bronze frame.

"Our friend the Count must occasionally entertain house guests," Ethredge said significantly. "He is very sure of himself!"

The second room was smaller. Its furnishings were meager; a footman's uniform hung in an otherwise empty closet; the chest drawers revealed only a few odds and ends of soiled clothing.

It was unquestionably the room belonging to the idiot who had admitted Ethredge that first afternoon…

Only two locked doors remained, and with the shattering of the first the search came to an abrupt end. Behind its violated sanctuary, his attenuated, faultlessly dressed figure outstretched upon the counterpane, lay Count Woerz, asleep…

Ethredge crossed the room in swift, noiseless strides; he had glimpsed a square of monogrammed notepaper pinned against Count Woerz's snowy shirtfront. His hand swept downward, ripped the bit of paper from Woerz's breast.

It bore a brief message, written in Count Woerz's crabbed hand, and addressed to Commissioner Ethredge. That stark message read:

Commissioner Ethredge! Do not act with undue precipitance. Communicate with your fiancée. She sleeps. I alone can rouse her.

Leopold Woerz.

The terse note dropped from Ethredge's fingers. He whirled, looked about the room, saw the telephone set in its recess at the head of the bed. His shaking fingers dialed Mary's familiar number.

Ethredge, frantic, rasped a hoarse command. There was a long, long pause before at last the maid's voice, full of a strange, new fear, came back over the wire.

But Ethredge heard only the first words of her hysterical babble. The receiver had fallen from his fingers as from a bundle of nerveless sticks.

"Peters!" His agonized cry split through the room. "He's done something to Mary!" His eyes, bleak and suddenly cruel, stared down at the Count. "But I'm staying here until he awakes—if it takes a million years!"

CHAPTER TWENTY-ONE
The Vampires Awake

Twilight had come to the world beyond that apartment. And, in the instant of the sun's setting, Count Woerz had come awake!

The hiss of Peters' sharply indrawn breath warned Ethredge. As he turned, startled, he caught the spasmodic fluttering, the lifting of the sleeper's eyelids.

From the very second of waking Count Woerz's eyes were bright with complete comprehension, were calm with—was it contempt?

As if savoring to the uttermost his return to consciousness he seemed content momentarily to lie there without a gesture, with only the steady burning gaze of his eyes proclaiming the awakening of the unholy life within him. But then, slowly, his lips writhed in a thin smile.

"I expected you, Commissioner," he said, the calm, quiet words dripping menace. "I foresaw that you would come here. The fact that I am alive attests your chivalry. You found, of course, that all was not well with Mary, and now you wait, puzzling how you may force me to *free* her. Or, perhaps, you would bargain with me. Well, I listen."

Ethredge, like an avenging doom, looming over that great bed, opened his lips to speak. In that split second, warned by a red flash of triumph in Woerz's eyes, he wheeled, saw the downward sweep of a bludgeon against Peters' skull, heard the sickening crunch of metal against flesh and bone. The girl was leaping toward him; Count Woerz's animalesque chauffeur was rising from Peters' unconscious body. The girl was upon him, a raging, rending, demoniac fury. He threw up his hands to ward her off, felt his arms seized from behind by Count Woerz's hands, like talons of steel. And then the brutish chauffeur towered above him, the bludgeon that had beaten Peters down upraised.

God! He, too, was undead! His writhing lips were blood red!

And then consciousness exploded in a crashing inferno of cascading light and swooping darkness…

CHAPTER TWENTY-TWO
Mary Disappears

Ethredge, struggling upward through interminable layers of torture-filled darkness, awoke to brain-shattering pain. As the swirling mists began to clear from before his eyes he realized that he lay sprawled across Count Woerz's bed; on the crimson and gold rug Peters was trying, with excruciating slowness, to drag himself to his feet.

Ethredge saw Peters' blood-smeared face turn painfully toward him. "God, Peters," he muttered thickly, "they—" And then he remembered. Mary!

To the telephone, reeling, stumbling—to hear from the distant lips of an obviously relieved maid that Miss Roberts had roused, dressed, and, dismissing the sorely puzzled physician who was already in attendance, departed the house…

Ethredge softly set the telephone back in its cradle and turned to Peters, who had dragged himself to his feet and was now clinging, swaying like a drunken man, to the bedpost.

"Peters," he said hollowly, "she's gone!" But Peters' haggard eyes told him that he already guessed.

"We've got to find her!"

"We've got to find—both of them!" Peters grimly corrected.

But where to look? How to begin the search? Those were unanswerable questions. It was already obvious to Ethredge and Peters that the Count and his grisly retinue had fled, permanently. Nothing that had been left behind hinted where they might have gone.

Doggedly the Commissioner utilized the police teletype, ordered the exhumation of Katharine Grant's body. Behind the gloomy gray walls at Police Headquarters, with the whole machinery of the law in operation, he waited impatiently, together with Peters, for the break.

As the fruitless minutes slowly became hours, desperate yet powerless to act, they reviewed, over and over again, from every angle, the incredible case.

One inexplicable circumstance puzzled them. Time after time they returned to it, as though they sensed that in its solution lay an important key to the mystery.

Why had Count Woerz appeared at Mrs. Moore's bazaar? Why had he spent that hour in the Tent of the Past, the Present, and the Future?

CHAPTER TWENTY-THREE
Aboard the Yacht Cynthia

THE hours passed… Word came from Rosedale Cemetery that Katharine Grant's grave had been opened. The vault had been despoiled; the casket was empty…

The big, ugly clock set high on the wall above the Commissioner's desk slowly ticked away the minutes; it was long past midnight. The night crept onward into the small hours. The city slept.

"Peters! Peters!" Ethredge reiterated, again and again, his hands knotting and unclasping helplessly, "if we could only know *why* Woerz played the fortuneteller at Mrs. Moore's bazaar, when in all other things he attempts to appear normal, inconspicuous! What supremely important mission brought him there?"

And then he remembered. That slender, dark man with the livid scar on his left cheek…

"Peters!" he rasped. "That night at the bazaar—while you were sick—when I went to get whiskey for you, I saw a man come from the gypsy tent—a man who didn't seem dazed, a man who seemed singularly unaffected. Why didn't that man react as the others had done? Why, Peters? Can it be because Woerz didn't attempt to read his mind at all; can it be because business of a different nature was transacted within the security of that tent?"

Peters leaped to his feet. "Eichelman's pearls!" he shouted. "Describe the man, Commissioner!" And with the Commissioner's word-picture he nodded.

"Beniati," he said. "Without a doubt, Angelo Beniati." He smiled his satisfaction. "One of the cleverest fences in the world. Too bad you didn't recognize him." He frowned, puzzled. "But—the Moores! What brings the Moores into the picture? Influence? Beniati does not need influence, except, perhaps, in getting from country to country."

Ethredge's clenched fist crashed against the desk.

"Moore's yacht!"

Peters' eyes were glowing with fierce exultation as he slowly rose. "Moore's yacht!" he echoed. "The explanation! Beniati and those pearls are aboard Moore's yacht, bound for some foreign port where the string can be broken up and sold."

Ethredge had seized the telephone, "The harbor commission!"

The information he sought was easily obtained. Weston B. Moore's yacht, the *Cynthia*, had passed quarantine at eight-forty p.m…

Ethredge's eyes swept the face of the clock; his lips moved silently as he made a swift calculation.

"Eight hours!" he whispered. "Eight hours' start, and that yacht can do twenty-four knots! And they're headed for any port at all on the face of the earth. But Woerz is aboard. That is a certainty. Otherwise Beniati would have put to sea earlier in the day. When Woerz saw you at the bazaar he became frightened. He held Beniati in port. That yacht meant—escape!"

He towered erect, his face stony with resolution. "I'm chartering a seaplane, Peters, if I can get a pilot who'll fly me! I'm going after them!"

His hands swept up the telephone.

"I'm flying a circle over the Atlantic until I cross their path!"

Peters' fingers lightly caressed the service automatic at his hip. "Boy! I'm going with you!" he shouted.

CHAPTER TWENTY-FOUR
The Pursuit of the Cynthia

The long rays of the setting sun lay across the water, extending far into the east in a broad band of gold. Already the sky was perceptibly purpling; within half an hour the sun would set.

Through five tedious, racking hours an antedated amphibian had plunged into the north and east, her pilot-owner grimly intent on every motor sound, Ethredge and Peters watching every smudge of smoke that showed in all that expanse of water below.

They were almost five hundred miles from the nearest land.

Quietly Ethredge spoke.

"The seeing won't last much longer, Peters. In the east it's blurry, and in the west the sun's blinding." He touched the pilot's shoulder. "Charley!"

The pilot, a fanatically earnest young man who had known very well that in taking this charter he was also taking his life in his hands, looked up.

"Swing to the south; cut across the steamship lanes. Keep her that way until the seeing's gone."

Obediently the youngman, without a change of expression, kicked right rudder. Low down on the horizon, the magnified ball that was the sun swung from a position slightly to the right of their tail to a new station, its glow lancing along the right wing. The clouds shifted.

The dry, thunderous roar of twin Wasp motors; three men, taut with strain; the great bowl of the ocean; the slowly sinking furnace of the sun!

The sun's edge was a finger's breadth above the water when Ethredge saw the thin plume of black smoke, like a tiny, sooty feather, standing on the horizon far to the south.

"Give her the gun, Charley; there's a ship ahead!"

The dry beat of the motors increased; the miles vanished beneath the speeding amphibian in an unheeding desert of watery waste; the sooty feather became a long streamer of coal-smoke marching across an arc of ocean. A wobegone tramp steamer climbed into view beneath the pillar of smoke, the red lead on her belly showing at intervals in the slow heave of the sea.

Charley, the young pilot who that day was gambling his life against the dollars that would buy him an infinitesimal interest in some perky little airline, sent the plane skimming the long rollers in the lee of the tramp, which lay supine, the smoke lazily drifting from one rusted funnel, waiting. The plane settled, bit into the slowly heaving waves, bounced along in a shower of spray.

Ethredge, climbing out upon a wing, hailed a man in a vizored cap who leaned over the bridge of the tramp, a man with stubbly whiskers who sucked an unlighted pipe.

"Have you sighted a yacht, white, one funnel, the *Cynthia?*"

"*Cynthia? Cynthia?* Didn't catch the name, but we sartinly crossed a white yacht a bit back. Boilin' along nice, too."

But Ethredge was executing a fantastic sort of dance on the broad wing of the plane. "You're the *Nancy Moran,* out of Baltimore?" he yelled. "You'll get a gold watch from me for this, captain!"

The plane was swinging about, lumbering into the wind. Ethredge had disappeared within the cabin.

"Damned fools!" the captain of the *Nancy Moran* commented, as he watched the plane lift and dwindle into the east.

CHAPTER TWENTY-FIVE
A Stratagem

Ethredge and Peters, twelve thousand feet above the tremendous circle of ocean, simultaneously sighted the *Cynthia*, a tiny white arrowhead at the apex of miles of wake.

Ethredge was feverishly writing a message. Finished, he taped it about the handle of a wrench.

"That should bring Beniati up short," Peters gloated.

"I don't know," Ethredge replied somberly. "Beniati knows that we have no authority on the high seas."

The amphibian screamed downward; the white arrowhead grew from a toy ship to a millionaire's plaything, a faint eddy of superheated air from her diesel motors visible above her single pearly funnel. The amphibian roared across the knife-like prow of the yacht; the weighted note hurtled downward, bounded along the deck. A dark, scarred man was running from the bridge to pick it up. Beniati!

The plane was swinging about in a wide circle. The men on the *Cynthia's* bridge were arguing.

"The captain wants to stop the ship, and Beniati won't let him," Peters guessed. "Who'll win? The captain's master, but Beniati has authority from Moore..."

Minutes passed. And the *Cynthia*, her bows rising and falling slightly as she knifed through the greenish seas, plowed stubbornly ahead.

The muscles along Ethredge's jaws were ribbed, hard as rock.

"Charley." There was a curious, eager resonance in his voice. "Do you think you can set us down across that yacht's bows so that she'll have to run us down?"

The stripling pilot looked up briefly. "It can be done." A half-smile flickered across his face.

Musingly Ethredge went on, Most ship captains are pretty fine… We'll take the chance. And twenty thousand dollars to you, my lad—all the money I can raise in the world—if we see shore alive. *Put her down!"*

The boy piloting that plane licked his lips. Lower and lower the plane settled, until she was only a scant forty feet above the long green billows. And then she struck, lifted, struck again in a shower of spume. She was plowing ahead heavily, directly across the *Cynthia's* bows.

Charley, the pilot, cut his motors, leaped to escape the cabin.

In the sudden silence Ethredge and Peters, standing on the wing, could hear, plainly, the clang of the engine-room telegraph as the *Cynthia's* captain tried to swerve his ship. But the momentum of the heavy yacht was too great. A rushing wall of white, the incoherent sound of shouting men, and then came the crash, the dry snapping of propeller blades, the crunching groan of a crushed wing.

The little amphibian had suddenly vanished.

Three men, swimming in the Atlantic, and a white yacht slowly moving away.

But, ahead, the forward momentum of the *Cynthia* was slowly halting. Water turgidly boiling at her stern told that her engines had been reversed.

The *Cynthia's* captain was showing himself a man.

CHAPTER TWENTY-SIX
The Horror on the Yacht

A RAGING, fuming captain confronted the three dripping men as they were hauled aboard the *Cynthia*. And behind him stood another man, sleek, slender, with a scarred face. Beniati!

"Police!" Ethredge snapped, cutting short the captain's bellows. With a flick of his wrist he displayed his badge. "That man is an international jewel thief!"

"It's a lie!" Beniati screamed. His hand flashed within his coat, and appeared again clutching an ugly automatic.

With the speed of a striking serpent the *Cynthia's* captain's fist crashed against the gun, sent it skidding twenty feet down the deck. Beniati was rubbing his numbed wrist.

"You can't arrest me," he whimpered. "We're at sea. You have no authority here!"

The captain turned suddenly to his mate. "Lock him in his cabin," he ordered briskly. "This may cost me my job, but I'm going to get to the bottom of whatever's wrong. Your credentials, sir?"

Beniati, cursing and protesting, was led away...

Tersely, after he had identified himself, Ethredge snapped, "I want a list of your passengers. We are interested, particularly, in a tall, thin gentleman who came aboard last night just before you sailed. He is very probably sleeping."

Captain Halliday started. "Odd! But—Count Woerz; he is a nobleman—Count Woerz and his party are strange people, Commissioner. They remained in the lounge until almost daylight, and only went to their cabins at dawn; excepting, however, Count Woerz's servant, who retired early and who has been, you might say, guarding those cabins since sunrise. It is—peculiar…"

When Ethredge spoke his voice was hoarse and strange.

"Captain Halliday," he said slowly, "you have seen our credentials. We wish, now, to be shown to those cabins—and left alone."

Peters was examining his service automatic, which, as he had slipped from the wing of the foundering plane into the sea, he had protected as well as he could by holding it above his head. "All right, Commissioner," he said then, quietly. "Let's go."

COUNT WOERZ'S suite was abaft the lounge. There was a large living room facing the afterdeck, two master staterooms facing, respectively, to port and to starboard. Captain Halliday rapped briskly at the central door.

A moment's silence, and a guttural voice asked, "Who's there?"

"Captain Halliday. Open the door, please."

There was a long silence. Captain Halliday was whispering, "He came aboard yesterday morning, with baggage. He seems not too bright."

The hesitating shuffle of footsteps beyond the door. "You vill not come vithin?" the guttural voice asked, querulously. "I haf orders no one to admit."

"I will not come inside," Captain Halliday said soothingly.

The door opened a few inches, and the vacuous, blond face of the man who had first admitted Ethredge to Woerz's apartment appeared. There was a guttural imprecation.

But Peters' foot was in the crack; Ethredge's shoulder was against the panel. The door burst wide; a scuffle, a click, and the pudgy, blond idiot was in handcuffs. He had begun to tremble.

Peters pushed him through the door. "Put him in some safe place, captain," he snapped. "He's harmless, poor devil!"

The door closed…

"Mary!"

Ethredge was leaping across that spacious cabin toward a vast mauve overstuffed chair above which he had glimpsed the warm brown halo of a woman's hair.

"Mary! Oh Heaven!"

He had come close to her, had grasped her hands, was looking down with growing horror into her eyes which, wide open, stared through him with glassy intentness at the sea beyond the long window and the snowy rail.

"Hypnosis!" His anguished cry seared through the cabin.

"Ethredge!" It was Peters' voice, harsh, warning. Ethredge whirled. The door of one of the staterooms was softly opening.

Three persons came through that door—two men and a woman. The men were Count Woerz and his chauffeur; the girl was Katharine Grant!

The sun had set!

Through a single horrible instant all five stood tableauesque; only Mary, staring blindly over the twilight-shrouded ocean, did not tense. In that moment the beat of the engines seemed to Ethredge and Peters like the pounding of giant sledges upon mountains of metal.

Ethredge's right hand had slipped within his breast; Count Woerz's chauffeur had moved with pantherine quickness to a position commanding the door; Katharine Grant, wistfully girlish-looking in flaring white trousers and sports jacket had, with seeming unconcern, seated herself in one of the deep lounge chairs and was quietly watching Ethredge; Count Woerz himself had not moved.

Rage like a hot, thin fire and a something, too, that may have been fear, were in Count Woerz's voice as he spoke.

"I had not expected you to follow me here, Commissioner Ethredge. You are more brilliant than I supposed. I should have killed you. Yet—your sweetheart sleeps. I offer you terms."

Ethredge stood motionless, his chin sunk on his breast. Then, "To hell with your terms!" he said softly. "If Mary could know, she would have me do as I am doing. I am going to kill you!" His fist, within his coat, had suddenly knotted.

Count Woerz smiled thinly. "Your gun is useless," he said significantly. "But now—guard the door, Sebastian!"

He sprang, his fingers outstretched like the talons of some ghastly bird of prey. Ethredge's hand flicked from his coat with the speed of light.

"Not a gun, Woerz!" he hissed, *"but the dagger that killed Eichelman!"* The knife gleamed dully through a swift lunging arc.

Woerz had swerved desperately, trying to halt his plunging rush—too late. The knife ripped down through his coat, shearing his arm from shoulder to elbow.

Woerz reeled back. His eyes were suddenly glaring redly, hot with fear, like the eyes of a trapped beast. Blood gushed from his wounded arm, down across his reddening fingers, to the rug.

"Sebastian," he gasped. "The knife!"

The ape-like chauffeur lunged, evaded Ethredge's thrust with simian agility; his fingers gripped the Commissioner's wrist, twisted. The blood-tipped knife dropped to the floor.

Woerz chuckled, a sound of unutterable evil and horror. Swiftly he stooped to pick up the dagger. And in that instant, he staggered, slumped to his knees, an expression of incredulous amazement and mortal fear on his face.

A spot of crimson had jutted abruptly upon his left breast!

Behind Ethredge, Peters' automatic was barking; two shots in rapid succession. Count Woerz's chauffeur spun drunkenly as the slugs jerked into his body, then reeled and pitched forward on his face.

Katharine Grant, her face a nightmare of unhuman hate, had leaped from her chair and was springing across the few feet that separated her from Peters. She never crossed that strip of rug.

Aiming at her softly youthful breast with the calmness of one who practices target shooting, Peters, an expression of unutterable pain in his eyes, sent a single shot into her heart.

In that instant the room was full of a scream of terror. Ethredge and Peters whirled.

That scream had come from Mary's throat!

For Mary was awake. She stood there swaying, her face white with horror and bewilderment.

"Charles! Charles!" she gasped. "Behind you!"

She had fainted. The sounds of pounding, of excited oaths came through the door.

Ethredge turned, to open the door—and clutched his throat while his senses reeled.

On that superb rug lay the dehydrated body, the formaldehyde-saturated body of a girl many months dead; her complexion purpled and saffron, her cheeks sunken, her half-opened eyes masses of putrefaction. And, a few feet away, the clothes lying loosely about them, a gray pus mingled with red blood dribbling from naked bones, lay two skeletons.

Peters, his face ashen, was moaning inanely, "God! How can I tell Maggie that I had the ballistics boys melt up her solid silver spoons!"

CHAPTER TWENTY-SEVEN
Buried at Sea

The moon, two handbreadths above the eastern rim of the world, sent her rays lancing across the black ocean, transforming the *Cynthia's* wake into a silvered, enchanted roadway. The heavens were a lake of stars.

Ethredge, Peters, and Mary Roberts sat close together on the *Cynthia's* afterdeck. They were warmly bundled in greatcoats, for it was close to midnight and the night was unseasonably cold. They were conversing in low tones, with long silences. Their faces, white in the moonlight, still showed traces of the horror that had been.

"And so," Peters said softly, "the Eichelman case is solved."

He lifted the fabulously valuable string of pearls from their box, lying on a table at his elbow, let them gleam and shimmer in the moonlight for a moment before putting them down. "Too bad you can't keep these for Mary, Charles."

"Yes," Ethredge laughed. "And the other jewels, and the bonds. But those things all go to Eichelman's estate."

He was silent for a moment.

"Mary and I don't need Eichelman's pearls to be—happy."

She lifted his hand between her warm little fingers, touched it gently with her lips. Silence, like a canopy of friendship, fell upon the three...

"Yes," Peters mused, after a little time had passed, "it's best that we—buried them at sea. No one would ever believe."

"No," Ethredge agreed. "Only those aboard this yacht will ever know what really happened. They will be silent."

Peters laughed dryly. "They'd be afraid people'd think them soft-headed," he said, with sage wisdom.

Ethredge drew Mary's head closer down against his shoulder.

"It's best that the Grants never know that we opened—Katharine's grave," he mused. "Too bad, of course, that we can't prosecute Beniati and Moore."

"Well, we can't," Peters said flatly. "We'd be ridiculed out of town."

The old, whimsical smile flickered across Ethredge's face.

"Yes," he admitted. "About all we can do is put that poor devil of a servant of Woerz's in some comfortable asylum. Funny that Woerz would use an idiot."

Peters shook his head. "He *had* to use an idiot. No sane man could have worked for him without instinctively feeling what he was. That idiot was a peasant—someone Woerz probably took from his own estate as a child."

Ethredge was squinting at the moon. "Nice moon tonight, Peters," he said, presently.

Peters grinned and rose. "Well," he said, "I can take a hint. Guess I'll get the steward to bring some of Moore's Scotch to my cabin. It isn't often that I have a chance to raid a millionaire's liquor. Good-night—Charles—Mary…"

The sound of his footsteps receded down the deck. The steady thud of the engines, the rush of water against the hull, the whisper of the night wind, were a monotony of sound that might have been designed by the gods as an accompaniment to love. The moon was riding higher in the heavens; the ocean was flecked and banded with silver.

Ethredge turned to his sweetheart, looked down into her moon-bathed face. His lips touched her mouth; his arms went about her shoulders.

He drew her close…

THE END

If you've enjoyed this book, you will not want to miss these terrific titles…

ARMCHAIR SCI-FI & HORROR DOUBLE NOVELS, $12.95 each

D-211   **PLANET OF EXILE** by Edmond Hamilton
        BRAIN TWISTER by Randall Garrett & Laurence M. Janifer

D-212   **LORELEI OF THE RED MIST** by L. Brackett & Ray Bradbury
        GOLD IN THE SKY by Alan E. Nourse

D-213   **NEXT DOOR TO THE SUN** by Stanton A. Coblentz
        MARTIAN NIGHTMARE by Bryce Walton

D-214   **THE OSILANS** by Arthur J. Burks
        THE METAL MONSTER by E. K. Jarvis

D-215   **LIFE EVERLASTING** by David H. Keller, M. D.
        FOREVER WE DIE by Milton Lesser

D-216   **SECRET OF THE FLAMING RING** by Rog Phillips
        THE SECRET MARTIANS by Jack Sharkey

D-217   **THE CRUCTARS ARE COMING** by Paul Lawrence Payne
        MADE TO ORDER by Frank Belknap Long

D-218   **SEVEN FROM THE STARS** by Marion Zimmer Bradley
        THE GIRL WHO READ MINDS by Robert Moore Williams

D-219   **DAWN TO DUSK** by Eando Binder
        BEAST-MEN OF CERES, THE by Aladra Septama

D-220   **THE TERRIBLE PUPPETS** by Paul W. Fairman
        THE COSMIC GEOIDS by John Taine

ARMCHAIR MASTERS OF SCIENCE FICTION SERIES, $16.95 each

MS-11   **MASTERS OF SCIENCE FICTION, Vol. Eleven**
        Robert Silverberg: The Ace Novels, Part One

MS-12   **MASTERS OF SCIENCE FICTION, Vol. Twelve**
        Robert Silverberg: The Ace Novels, Part Two

ARMCHAIR MYSTERY-CRIME DOUBLE NOVELS, $12.95 each

B-41   **LAUGHTER CAME SCREAMING** by Henry Kane
        THE EXTORTIONERS by Ovid Demaris

B-42   **THEY ALL RAN AWAY** by Edward Ronns
        BACKFIRE by Floyd Mahannah

B-43   **BLOOD OF MY BROTHER** by Stephen Marlowe
        THE GUILTY BYSTANDER by Mike Brett

B-44   **MURDER WITHOUT TEARS** by Leonard Lupton
        NO WAY OUT by Milton K. Ozaki

If you've enjoyed this book, you will not want to miss these terrific titles…

ARMCHAIR SCI-FI & HORROR DOUBLE NOVELS, $12.95 each

D-221   **UNDER VENUSIAN FLAGS** by Nelson S. Bond
        BLOOD ON MY JETS by Algis Budrys

D-222   **CITIES IN THE AIR** by Edmond Hamilton
        THE WAR OF THE PLANETS by Harl Vincent

D-223   **MISTRESS OF MACHINE-AGE MADNESS** by Jack Williamson
        THE IMPOSSIBLES by Randall Garrett & Laurence M. Janifer

D-224   **WALL OF FIRE** by Charles Eric Maine
        TOO MANY WORLDS by Gerald Vance

D-225   **THE VEILED WOMAN** by Mickey Spillane & Howard Browne
        PELLUCIDAR by Edgar Rice Burroughs

D-226   **LOOT OF THE VAMPIRE** by Thorp McClusky
        THE MAN WHO MADE MANIACS by Jim Harmon

D-227   **COLOSSUS** by S. J. Byrne
        ISLE OF DOOM by Robert Moore Williams

D-228   **RETURN OF CREEGAR** by David Wright O'Brien
        EIGHT KEYS TO EDEN by Mark Clifton

D-229   **THE TIMELESS MAN** by Robert Donald Locke
        ENEMY OF THE QUA by Dwight V. Swain

D-230   **THE MAN THE TECH-MEN MADE** by Fox B. Holden
        A WORLD HE NEVER MADE by Edwin Benson

ARMCHAIR SCIENCE FICTION CLASSICS, $12.95 each

C-77   **THESE ARE MY CHILDREN**
        by Rog Phillips

C-78   **STRANGER SUNS**
        by George Zebrowski

C-79   **THE SECOND DELUGE**
        by Garrett P. Serviss

ARMCHAIR SCI-FI & HORROR GEMS SERIES, $12.95 each

G-27   **SCIENCE FICTION GEMS, Vol. Fourteen**
        Robert Moore Williams and others

G-28   **HORROR GEMS, Vol. Fourteen**
        Manly Banister and others

HE HAD BEEN KILLED—SO WHY WAS HE STILL ALIVE?

Jace Reid had felt the impact of the bullet. He had remembered falling face downwards into the dirt. The next thing he knew he was reading about his own death, while lying on a bed in an institute for the insane. It had started with a picture of himself making love to a girl, and a threatening phone call—then his own startling death! The police had the body—there could be no doubt that it was Jace Reid. But then, who was he? Carla said he was immortal and of the Un-dead. A vampire. And even in his arms she called him the Master. The Master of what? And what about those nightmares? The strangled cat? The idol? And most of all—who were the Chosen Ones?

A shocking story of horror and intrigue, set against the background of a depraved cult of sadism…

CAST OF CHARACTERS

JACE REID
His life as a freelance writer would lead him into the eye-opening world of sadistic rituals and perverted cults.

CARLA MACNITER
She was evil to the core and the only way to stem her pursuit of madness was either to cure her…or to kill her.

LISA TANNER
Under that beauty and brains was a woman who would stop at nothing to help her client…and lover.

LT. OSLOW
As a police officer he had two driving motivations: to take down the perverted satanic cults and to find his wife's killer.

DORIS MACNITER
She had been mentally and emotionally controlled by her sister, twisted into a hodgepodge of the best and worst of both of them.

SGT. GRUBBS
In the heat of the moment this level-headed, no-nonsense police Sergeant was often just what the Force needed.

THE MAN WHO MADE MANIACS!

By JIM HARMON

ARMCHAIR FICTION
PO Box 4369, Medford, Oregon 97504

*For more information about Armchair Books and products, visit our
website at…*

www.armchairfiction.com

Or email us at…

armchairfiction@yahoo.com

CHAPTER ONE

They were looking at each other over a six o'clock cigarette, smiling a little in anticipation of what they knew was coming next, when the indigo scene was shattered with a shock.

It's a hell of a time for the phone to ring, Jace Reid thought grimly as he picked up the ivory receiver.

"Hello, Hello, hello," he said.

"Hi, boy." The whisper grated like an onion through a salad machine. "We all want you to know we think you swing like the greatest."

"Who is this? How did you get this number?"

"We like your number. We liked that little number in the picture, the one with the big baloozas. We liked what you did with that razor, then, man. That was a real jolt."

"I'm glad you liked the picture. However, this phone is reserved for business purposes only, and I would appreciate it if you didn't call me again."

"But Jace, I did call you on business," the voice insinuated. "The kind of business you like. See, we got these chicks that like to be hurt. Ever really slammed a naked girl around with a rubber hose and taught 'em what a man was good for? Of course, you realize you don't want to kill off your fun, even—"

"Look!" Reid shouted, a vein in his head throbbing, "will you kooks understand once and for all I'm not interested in your orgies? I wrote a book and a motion picture that was a clinical study of a pair of sex fiends, yes, but 'Maniacs' is a subject I'm interested in only on the screen, not off."

"You're off," the voice snickered. "You're off all that kind of stuff. Sure, I know. But think about a nice juicy pair of baloozas, and taking a nice, handy length of orange crate slat and—"

Reid dropped the receiver like a rotten salmon. He picked up his stub of a cigarette from the ashtray, burned his fingers and took a drag that would have turned the A. M. A. pale.

Lisa Tanner remained comfortably curled on the couch, her legs accentuated by being half concealed under her body. She dusted an imaginary cigarette ash from her cleavage and sat up straighter. There was no effort wasted to disguise the fact that she was a tall redhead. No sexless low heels went with the emerald frock of lone, graceful line. Reid was tall himself.

We make a good pair, he thought, she's beautiful, and they tell me I'd be handsome if I smiled. He decided he would try it sometime. Sometime later.

"Another kook?" Lisa watched his nod. "Why don't you have your number changed? It would cost money but you can afford it now."

"I'm not going to let those weirdo's put me on the run. I'll stick 'em out."

"And get 'em chopped off," Lisa said. "That isn't a very practical attitude."

"You worry about me too much."

"Would you rather I worried about somebody else?"

"No," he said.

Lisa rubbed out her cigarette and crossed to the window. She had a nice silhouette and she knew it.

"I do worry about you, Jace. You're taking this too hard. You're letting all these people on the lunatic fringe get under your skin. If they bother you that much, take out your phone and let somebody check your mail for you."

"I wrote the damned picture," Reid stormed. "I'm not trying to deny it. I'm the creator of sex fiends, the maker of maniacs. I'm not trying to chicken out of it."

"Aren't you?" Lisa asked. "Sounds to me like you are making a confession and asking for absolution."

"Okay, you wise broad, so I do have some guilt feelings about Maniacs. Guilt feelings, not a guilt complex. Remember the guy who killed the babysitter in Chicago after he saw the picture?"

"Jace, you know he would have killed the girl after seeing *Mickey Mouse Go To Mars*. He was in a mood for killing, so he went to see a picture about killing. That wasn't enough to satisfy him—sometimes it is—so he had to go and kill for himself."

"You're logical and reasonable, Lisa. Like always, Lisa. But I don't operate quite that orderly. I can realize the truth of what you say intellectually, but emotionally, I wonder, just a little."

"You worry too much," she said. "Why don't we go to bed?"

She came and leaned against him, her body blending against his from habitual knowledge of the curves and recesses.

"You think I need to get to sleep?" Reid asked.

"Um-hmm," she answered. "And I intend to see to it that you do."

He touched the hollow of her throat with his tongue, and her nails bit through his jacket.

The doorbell stabbed at them insistently.

Reid released her and turned, making a brief but eloquent curse.

Lisa smiled and petted his cheek.

He went to the door and opened it.

The well-dressed, middle-aged man showed him what appeared to be a driver's license until Reid noticed the gold badge fastened to the other hinge of the leather case.

"Good evening. Police business. I'm Lieutenant Oslow. Are you Jace Reid?"

"Yes, that's right. Won't you step in, Lieutenant? What's the trouble?"

Oslow stepped inside and Reid closed the door after him. The Lieutenant took off his snap-brim hat.

"Mrs. Reid?" Oslow asked.

"Lisa Turner, my agent. Lisa, Lieutenant Oslow."

Lisa smiled charmingly. "Lieutenant."

"What did you say this was about, Lieutenant?" Reid asked, offering a chair.

Oslow stood. "I didn't say, Mr. Reid, but it's a homicide matter."

"I'm supposed to be an expert on murder, but only the fictional ones."

"An expert; yes. Well, sir, we have in custody a man who has just confessed to the brutal murder of a young schoolteacher. And he says you gave him the whole idea."

"I was expecting something like this." Then noticing the heightened interest in Onslow's part, he added, "He claims he got the idea after seeing my picture, right?"

"Wrong. He claims that you are the head of, a sadism cult, and that you personally gave him the orders to go out and murder this girl."

"Ye gods," Reid mumbled, realizing the shock on Lisa's face must be mirrored on his own. "Why would the poor screwball want to say a thing like that?"

"You're an expert," Oslow said, an unexpected glint in his eye. "You know how it is. These beginners and their professional jealousy."

*   *   *

The car droned on through the sluggish Los Angeles traffic with Oslow locked to the steering wheel, his hard eyes straight ahead.

Reid sat beside him, feeling only half-awake. He had written about policemen and squad cars hundreds, if not thousands, of times, but this was the first time he had been in one since he ran away from home as a boy. He could hardly believe Oslow was serious. He almost expected this to turn out to be some kind of elaborate joke.

Almost, but not quite.

"Lieutenant," Reid said, parting the layers of silence, "what do you know about this sex-sadism cult I'm accused of being connected with?"

"Quite a bit, as a matter of fact," Oslow said. "I've made kind of a special investigation of this sort of thing."

"I can't understand why these loonies would pick me out to involve in their activities."

Oslow shrugged, half-smiling. "Famous people are always getting picked on by crackpots. Don't worry about it. If you aren't really involved, they can't hurt you."

"I'm being dragged off to a police station, Lieutenant! That's not doing me any good."

"Take it easy. Going to a police station once in your life won't hurt you any, Mr. Reid."

"That's what they told Al Capone. I don't like it very much, I'll tell you that."

The policeman shifted his eyes from the road a second. "Maybe you don't like me much either, Mr. Reid. Cops never win personality polls. I'm just doing my job. Don't take this thing personal."

"I'm not blaming you for this, lieutenant," Reid said, wondering if he really had been. "But nobody likes being dragged out of a comfortable home by a policeman…"

"And being taken away from a good-looking woman like Miss Tanner, huh?"

He stiffened. "Now you're getting personal. Let's leave Miss Tanner out of this."

"No offense. No offense."

Reid slouched back in his seat. "That's what I keep telling you I've committed…no offense."

The engine purred on without interruption for a few more close-packed city miles.

Reid took a deep breath. "Look, lieutenant, we sort of got off the subject back there. You were going to tell me about these sex cults."

Oslow's face-hardened in the neon light coming through the windshield as they paused for a red light. "Yeah, I was, wasn't I? Well, as you may know…" (Reid didn't like the implied accusation there) "…there is just about any kind of sex perversion you could want in Los Angeles County. The male homosexuals are an active and powerful force, infiltrated everywhere. They help elect a lot of politicians. The lesbos aren't far behind them. Somebody once said that one out of every four attractive women in Hollywood is sleeping with the other three."

Reid nodded. "Sometimes not singly either."

Oslow chuckled. "You got an active imagination. But the sadists and masochists are the worst. At least, as a police problem. They physically hurt themselves, each other—and innocent people. I know."

The writer studied the officer's face. Yes, he knew a lot about hurting and pain—coming and going, it looked like.

"How do they hurt themselves?" Reid asked.

"You name it. They want to punish themselves for something, so they really will do anything to cause themselves pain. Of course, it isn't really pain to them—it's pleasure."

"Sure. I know a little something about psychology. Layman's knowledge. But what exactly do they do? Is a murder like this the usual sort of thing for these cultists?"

Oslow shook his head. "No. Most of the cults are run by somebody—usually some old guy with a beard claiming to have supernatural powers. He doesn't want the police down on him so he usually keeps his flock from killing each other or bothering outsiders at all. They just—"

"Yes, just what do they do?"

"You seem very interested, Mr. Reid?"

"Why shouldn't I be interested?" Reid said warmly. "I'm accused of telling these goons what to do. I'd like to know what I'm supposed to be telling them."

"Well, mostly it's pretty mild and harmless. They spank each other with paddles or bamboos or whips. Nothing much. Sometimes it gets out of hand when one of them can't stop, when he simply has to—"

A look swept across Oslow's face as if he had just remembered something.

"Say, Mr. Reid, we're going to have to stop the car for a moment. I have to telephone my partner, Sergeant Grubb, on a police matter."

Reid glanced at the dials on the dashboard. "Can't you use the radio?"

"That's a police radio, not a civilian radiophone. Grubb will be near a regular telephone. It will just take a moment. I'll stop at the next drugstore. I know you're anxious to get this bit of business out of the way."

"I can't say I am too anxious to get into jail. Make your phone call. Don't worry about delaying me in the slightest."

Oslow wheeled the car to the curb, parking in a red curb area.

There are some advantages to being a policeman, Reid thought fleetingly.

The lieutenant shut off the motor. "Why don't you come in with me and have a cup of coffee on me while I phone? Might help relax you a bit."

No, of course, Reid realized. I can't be left alone in the car.

They got out opposite sides and walked on into the drugstore. Inside, Oslow motioned to a phone booth in the back near the soda fountain.

They walked past the display of Yardley's, chocolate-covered cherries, and Kotex, and took the corner stool.

Oslow slapped his palm down on the counter and lifted it, revealing a dime. "Coffee's on me."

The policeman went over to the glass-enclosed booth and shut the door, facing in Reid's direction as he dialed.

Has to keep me in sight at all times, he thought.

"Did Oslow say coffee for you, mister?"

He looked up at the waitress. For a change, this one was worth looking at. Her breasts punched out the front of her blue uniform very attractively and reddish glints in her brown hair looked natural.

"Yes, coffee," he said absently.

The girl turned around. That was good, too. She turned back and sat his coffee mug in front of him.

"Would you like a doughnut, too?"

"No, thanks."

"Go ahead! It's on the house."

"*What?* Why?"

"Well," the girl said reluctantly, "the food down there isn't the greatest thing in the world. And anyway, maybe you'd kind of like to have your strength up."

"Now wait a minute—just what do you think?" Reid asked, a sinking sensation filling him he knew what she was thinking.

"Look, honey," the girl said, "I know who and what Oslow is. There are only two kinds of guys he would come in here with and buy coffee for and you don't look like a cop."

"That's right," he said. "I'm not a cop." If she were wrong, how *far* was she wrong. He was being brought in by a cop, wasn't he? Just one more aggravation he had got himself into since coming to Hollywood.

"I bet you didn't do it," the girl said impulsively, leaning her elbows on the counter.

Her large breasts flowed out and almost touched the polished black surface area. Maybe it was a fetish, but if there was anyone thing Reid admired in a woman it was a good big well-shaped pair of breasts. He had trouble keeping from looking at them all the time.

"I know how it is," the girl went on. "You can be innocent and still get picked up by the cops." She hesitated a moment, then said impulsively, "I know. It happened to me."

"Really?" Reid said, finding himself somehow vaguely interested despite his own troubles.

"Sure. It's embarrassing—but I can tell you're a nice guy—they picked me up for soliciting. Imagine!"

"Incredible!" He tasted his coffee. Well, it had to be that way. They hired an attractive waitress to take your mind off the coffee.

"Sure. Look, if I wanted to hustle, you think I'd have to solicit anybody? I get enough offers in one night to keep me busy for a month of one-hour sessions."

"I don't doubt it."

"Sure. It's just that—well, I like men. What's wrong with that? A guy can go up to a girl he likes the looks of and make a little pass and if he's polite about it, it's okay. But brother, let a girl try the same thing on some attractive guy like you and you'd think she was John Wilkes Booth or somebody. I just saw this good-looking guy on the corner and I just went up and asked him for a light, and when this cop sees us, and I'm leaning *these* against him a little—"

But, for once, he wasn't looking at those. A crowd had formed between the phone booth and the fountain. There were lots of people that night that must have needed a lot of Yardley's or chocolate-covered cherries or even Kotex, he decided. But Oslow wouldn't like him getting out of sight.

Reid got off the stool, gave the sexy waitress a half-wave of his hand goodbye and started for the booth. He skirted around the crowd and finally saw the phone booth.

The booth was empty. Oslow was gone.

Reid blinked. Could it have been some kind of a hoax after all?

Fingers dug hard into his biceps.

"What are you doing over here by this *exit*, Mr. Reid?" Oslow asked.

"Looking for you," he answered.

"By the exit?"

"Yes. That's where you were, weren't you?"

"Come on. Let's get back to the car. You don't want to get around exits when somebody like me is escorting you, Mr. Reid. It makes us nervous."

He went with Oslow back to the car and climbed in.

Now it was full night. The lights made a gaudy canyon for them to pass through.

Reid looked at his driver. The man had been almost threatening back there.

A sudden—ridiculous—thought struck him.

How did he really know he was being taken to a police station?

How did he know *where* this hard relentless man was taking him?

CHAPTER TWO

Reid found himself shaking. God, how much did they expect him to go through? This was a tomb. He was in a tomb. Locked in alive. The walls were marble and impenetrable. How could anybody who was alive stay in a place like this?

What kind of sadists would put a man through something like this?

The police lieutenant's footsteps echoed hollowly as he marched back towards Reid.

"Sorry to have you wait out in the hall like this, Mr. Reid, but my office is being painted and I doubt if you'd like the interrogation rooms."

"What about this man who accused me of being an accessory to murder?" Reid said.

"Him?"

"Yes, him. What about him?"

"First of all, Mr. Reid, let me say how much I appreciate your cooperation," the lieutenant said. "You've certainly cooperated with us all the way. But you can see where it is to your advantage to get those things cleared up before the newspapers get a hold of him."

"Lieutenant, about the accusation—I want to know if I'm under suspicion of some crime?"

"Certainly not, sir!" Oslow said, giving a fair impression of being aghast at the thought. "It was only a wild accusation—"

"Then why do you come to me?" Reid demanded. "Would you arrest Dinah Shore if somebody accused her of making pornographic party records?"

"No, sir, but we might arrest certain actors on suspicion if we got reports of them using narcotics. A lot depends on reputation."

"You mean just because I write about sex murders, I can be suspected of one? Lieutenant, I once wrote a novel about Lesbians."

Oslow's features twitched slightly with impatience. "Mr. Reid, you must admit you have been in some rather strange circles lately. On research, no doubt, but still—"

"What kind of circles are you talking about?"

"Well, Mr. Reid, you don't want to stand in this stuffy hall all day. I came to tell you you can go on home now."

"Home?" Aren't I even going to get a chance to face the man who accused me of masterminding a murder?"

"No, sir. Nobody's going to face him but the psychiatrist. He could have possibly killed the schoolteacher. He was in the hospital for insulin shock at the time. One of those psychos who goes around seeking punishment, you know."

"Why would he want to have me punished with him?"

Reid slouched back wearily against a poster on the wall. Glancing up at the caption, he read: WE WANT YOUR BLOOD—GIVE NOW RED CROSS.

"Jealousy," Oslow explained. "Figures you're rich now, and being the kind of guy you are, you can have all the women you want to torture to death. He even made a drawing of your home the way he imagined it—iron maidens, and some juicier ones.

"But that's insane!"

"You must be right. He's in the psychiatric ward, isn't he?"

"What makes a man like that?" Reid wondered aloud.

"Well you're the expert, Mr. Reid. But I got my own ideas. It's our whole culture…" Oslow said, a trifle proud of his use of the word, "…it throws sex at us all the time—television, movies, books, magazines. Some guys can't handle that much sex."

"But lieutenant, we're all so repressed it's some relief to experience sex vicariously," Reid said.

"You're probably right. Just the same—some guy just go nuts when they see a nice pair of baloozas."

Baloozas, Reid thought. Odd word. It's meaning clear, of course. But he had only heard it recently for the first time… That crackpot telephone call! The whispering, disguised voice.

Oslow shook his head. "Yes, sir, a pair of baloozas and they're set off. They've got to have their 'fun'."

"Must be a hard job working with people like that," Reid managed.

Oslow met Reid's eyes squarely. "I have to do what I have to do. Actually, Mr. Reid, I find great satisfaction in it. You know how it is—a man takes pride in his work."

Reid put his bare palm on the stonewall. There was a considerable difference in temperature, but the stone began to warm his flesh. "Yes. Well, goodbye."

Reid turned on his heel and went down the hall towards the dismal patch of winter-gray twilight at its end.

"Be seeing you, Lieutenant Oslow called back."

*   *   *

"It's obvious what's going on," Lisa said over her pink lady.

Reid lowered his glass of barren rocks. "It is? I wish someone would explain it to me."

"One of these crackpots got hold of your name and telephone number somehow and is passing it around to all the rest of them," she said.

"That's encouraging," Reid said. "That's delightful. I can expect this thing to increase by geometric progression. Soon I'll be known to every sex fiend in the country and they will all be sending me invitations to join their parties or telling the police that each orgy was my personal idea."

"It's much too personal," she said thoughtfully.

"My idea?"

"No. Being a sex maniac is a solitary occupation. You know, like being a writer ("thanks" he interjected) so they won't all know each other to be able to pass your number along. Only the exceptions band together."

"Lightning hardly ever strikes anybody, but the exceptions can be fatal."

His punchline was underscored by the ringing of the doorbell.

"Right on cue," Lisa murmured. "Just like in a movie."

"That's what life is like," Reid said. "A movie. A bad movie. Or maybe it's more like television."

Reid started to answer the door, but a small ball of fluff got under his feet.

"I've got a headache, Lisa," Reid complained patiently. "That shrill doorbell is bad enough, but must you have that cat of yours stomping about the apartment?"

Reid scooted Angel aside with the edge of his Oxford.

He pulled back the door and drew up sharply. The girl on the threshold was incredibly appealing to him. Not so much her beauty, or perhaps it was that he knew himself well enough to know that what any man considers beauty is only a combination of his pet fetishes.

This girl had the breasts, lushy semi-conical; she had the eyes, dark, dissipatedly shadowed, healthily clear. And she had the grace and presence. Although he had never selected women by hair color, he was struck by her carefully styled hair, artful as treason, soft as pleasure, black as sin.

In short, the girl hit Reid right between the glands.

"What can I do for you?" Reid suggested.

"Mr. Reid?" she said. He liked her throaty voice, too. "Jace Reid?"

"That's right."

He noticed she was wearing clothes. A tanish suit. Who wears suits? Could she be one of those Literary Ladies? He didn't think he could stand it if she went into a long spiel about how she really wanted to explore his soul, how she really wanted to get into him.

"Mr. Reid," the girl said in a rush, "you've got to stop doing what you're doing to my sister. Her health won't permit it. It will *kill* her."

"What are you talking about?" he demanded. Oh, lord, another one. "What are you? Who is your sister?"

"My name is Doris MacNiter. My sister is Carla MacNiter."

"I've never met either of you in my life. You've made a mistake. Maybe some friend of your sister's has been using my name."

Since the movie had been released, things like this had been happening. He was developing a weary patience for them.

"It's *you,*" Doris said, her remarkable eyes flashing. "Who else but you could it be with her here?"

Doris opened her purse, whipped out a glossy photograph, thrust it at him.

Reid reluctantly accepted the picture and looked at himself and a brunet girl doing something unspeakably vile.

Reid's head ached and he felt dizzy and nauseous.

When was the last time I was drunk enough to do something like that? He looked at the picture again and shook his head. I was never, never that drunk in my life.

"Maybe you'd better come in," he said. "Don't worry. Miss Tanner, my agent, is here to chaperone us."

Doris' chin lifted defiantly and she stepped into the apartment.

Reid closed the door and locked it.

He grabbed the girl by the shoulders and hurled her down on the couch. Her eyes and mouth were open, and one shoe was off. She half-sat, half-lay on the couch, cowering back against the cushions.

"Remember," Lisa said, "I'm here to chaperone you."

"You can do something more useful," Reid said.

"You can call the police. I don't like to be blackmailed. Not with some faked photograph."

"*Fake?*" Doris said, choking back her hysteria. "*Faked?*" Look at the photograph, Mr. Reid. Just look at it closely. "How could it possibly be faked?"

Hesitating a moment, Reid crossed to his desk, snapped on the typing lamp and dug out a magnifying lens from the rubbish in his second drawer.

He studied the photograph under the strong glass. "It could be faked," he corrected. "It *must* be faked, but I don't think I could prove it. I did some research on 'paste-up' jobs like this for a story once. If expertly enough done, the 'paste-up' can't be spotted even under a microscope. The only way to prove fakery is to produce the original from which the pasted-in subject was cut. Then you have to prove that *this* was the original, not a paste-up itself. Of course, finding the original is impossible, if somebody just snapped your picture as you walked down the street, just for a case like this."

"That's no fake," Doris said bitterly. "My sister, Carla, showed it to me, bragged about it, rubbed my face in it. She's *proud* of it. But it can't go on. It will *kill* her. It would kill *any* woman."

"I would like to see that picture," Lisa pleaded.

"No," Reid said, but Lisa snatched it out of his hands.

"Humm," Lisa mused.

He looked at the photograph again over her shoulder. In the picture, he was beating a naked girl with a whip.

At first, he had thought the girl was Doris or her twin; but now he saw that the one in the photo didn't look much like Doris at all. Of course this girl's face and body were contorted in orgiastic ecstasy.

Reid's own expression in the picture was one of delicate precision, as if he were trying to lift a single grain of pollen from a rose with a pair of tweezers.

Behind them rose a figure—a statue—it *had* to be a statue, no question about it at all, *none*—a figure of some kind of creature with rivulets of blood drooling from its fangs to match the whelts on the girl's body.

"Pretty sick," Lisa commented briefly.

"Pretty slick, too," Reid added. "But I don't pay blackmail, Miss MacNiter."

Doris struggled with her face, and finally got it subdued, blinking back tears. "Mr. Reid, all I want you to do is leave Carla alone. She's sick, I know—she likes that sort of thing and she says I have no right to object to what two adults do in privacy. But this treatment—her health is failing. She can't go on."

"I've had just about—*enough.*"

Reid ripped the picture into confetti. "I know. You've got the negative. Turn it over to the newspapers, anything. Do your damnedest. Just get out of my home!"

He grabbed the girl by the arm and hustled her towards the door.

"You're evil, Mr. Reid!" Doris cried. "You're just as bad as the people you write about. If you weren't you couldn't write about them. And you're corrupting everybody you come in contact with, with your own madness, everybody you meet, everybody who reads your books, everybody who sees your movies..."

He shoved her out the door, slammed it, locked it, bolted it.

He leaned back against the door and shook inwardly.

"Don't let it get to you, baby," Lisa said in an infuriatingly motherly tone. "Just a bunch of crackpots got your name and phone number and photograph."

"Yes Lisa, yes. But where did they get those things? Who gave them my private unlisted number? I've been wondering about that. Who do you think it could be?"

"It could be anybody."

"Could it? I only know a limited number of 'anybody's'. I wonder—could it have been *you*, Lisa? Maybe you thought it would be a good publicity stunt. Maybe you wanted to get even with me for something."

"What for?" Lisa asked, her eyes flickering for only a second. "You've never got me into trouble. I sometimes doubt if you're even capable of it."

"Female!" he said. "You can get out, too. Just leave me alone. I'm beginning to think I can't trust anybody. Except myself."

"I wouldn't trust myself *too* far, Jace," Lisa said coolly, and walked out of the apartment.

I need a drink, he thought, and started for the bar at the other end of the paneled living room.

Halfway there, he swerved and went into the bedroom.

He collapsed on the bed and realized he was too tired to sleep. All he could do was lie there and think about his troubles, about...

Sleep.

CHAPTER THREE

Reid was dreaming and he knew he was dreaming.

He was dreaming horror.

Saturnalia.

He was alive in the years that followed the legendary founding of Rome in 753 B. C.

The festival had been lengthened from its original one day to a full week near the ebb of December.

Reid found himself in a purple toga, being served by his master, Paulus.

During this time of year the essential equality of all men was proved by the Masters serving the slaves.

The banquet table was fully as lavish and loaded with fruits, wine, and meats as any Reid had served himself.

"Broth!" Paulus called, his round face greasy with sweat. "You must have some warm broth, Master Reidus."

The fat figure waddled forward with a copper bowl of broth in his hands. The bowl seemed ingeniously hinged in the fat man's hands as it came over Reid's hip; it tilted and spilled the scalding liquid in a shimmering cascade.

Reid screamed.

"That's right, Reidus," Paulus said. "Make all the noise you want to. Today is your day."

"Ointment!" Reid called. "Master, an ointment! You must get it for me."

"Certainly, I must. Here, Slave Who is Master, here."

Reid lifted his toga and poured the ointment from the container Paulus had handed him.

He screamed.

"What? Wasn't vinegar what you had in mind? It is used as an ointment for the hair."

"Oh," Reid groaned, "will this day of freedom never be done?"

"Ah, you think of the night, do you? Of course, as my equal you shall have equal access to the women's quarters."

"No, Master," Reid pleaded. "I am free today and it is my free choice to leave your women alone."

"Nonsense," Paulus said. "You are free so you *must* make free with the women. I command it."

"You cannot. You are a slave. Slaves cannot command masters," Reid persisted.

"Little do you know, Reidus. Little do you know. Today is a day of freedom for me, too. A day when I may even forget how valuable you are. See, the veils are lifting. The women come."

Reid saw only one woman whom he recognized as Lysorla. No, he thought—that should be Lysorus. But it wasn't. It was Lysorla.

She walked proudly, he breasts and abdomen thrusting their femininity forward, her white legs scissoring through the wine-soaked mists. Her only garment was a low-slung Y-shaped girdle that accentuated her womanliness.

Reid's brain drowsed beneath the fumes of wine, so his body wakened quickly. He had seen and wanted her often. Now, for today, for Saturnalia, he would take her. And all her sisters he could find!

He brushed aside food and wine, pain and Master, and rushed toward the woman.

His hands found her flesh and her face writhing with pain and pleasure and changed to other faces, faces he had known and would know, and finally found the form of a great cat.

By some magic of Janus, he stood holding to one of the great cats bred for the arena.

Reid fought for his life, but of course, it was useless.

His fingers clamped down through fur and flesh and struck bone; they strangled and strangled…

But the cat's claws worked as they had been taught to work. The rear claws ripped and shredded and did their work.

There came a terrible slash and Reid knew he was no longer a man.

His fingers strangled…

Now he was disemboweled. His hands choked and choked.

The face before him was flowing and changing but relentlessly becoming the colorless featureless, timeless face of Death.

And the dream was over.

Or…the old dream of being Jace Reid, American, writer, human being, was beginning again.

He looked at the neat little strips of Hollywood sunlight sliced upon his bed sheet by the Venetian blinds and realized a new day was beginning.

Reid saw the dead cat lying on his chest. His hands were still locked around its neck.

He blinked. I killed Lisa's kitten. Angel. Poor little Angel.

Suddenly, he scrabbled aside the covers and stared at his body. No, no, that had only been part of the dream.

But the dead cat, that was real. He really had strangled the pitiful creature.

Suppose—suppose Lisa had been beside him?

What might have happened then?

He was a dangerous man when he was asleep.

He wasn't quite sane when he was awake, either. Would a sane man lie awake in bed holding a dead cat on his chest?

He shoved the dead kitten to the side of the bed and sat up, running his offending hands down over his chest.

I have to see a psychiatrist, he realized. No, a more basic part of him protested. No one must ever know about this. No one must ever know!

Something in the room with him shrieked. Finally, he realized, almost giggling with relief, that it was the telephone.

He wiped his wet palm on his pajama coat and lifted the received.

"So, Jace Reid," the woman's voice said, "you like to strangle cats to death, do you?"

*   *   *

He was still dreaming.

That was it.

He held to the phone and the idea of the dream for fully thirty seconds before he admitted he was awake and somebody knew what he had just done.

"What are you?" Reid demanded angrily.

No one had a right to know what a man did in the privacy of his bedroom; not even if it was strangling kittens.

"You know me, Jace. You know me. Doesn't my voice mean anything to you?"

"It means something to me."

"Yes, Jace—what does it mean?"

"I can't say it over the phone—it's against the law."

He wiped his hand across his face. Another famous Jace Reid wisecrack—that wouldn't solve anything. But who said he was good at solving his problems.

"Look," he demanded of the voice on the phone, "who are you? How can you see into my bedroom?"

"Then you admit that I can see what you've done?"

"You see it too accurately to deny the fact, I suppose. What is this? What's it all about?"

"You want to find out? You really want to find out?"

"Of course I do. Before I go nuts!"

"But you are mad, Jace, darling. Of course you are."

"Wait a minute now—I'm not crazy!"

"Sane men strangle cats, don't they?" the voice purred.

His fingers tightened on the telephone receiver.

As if he were trying to strangle— He broke off the thought.

"Okay, let's say I'm crazy. Crazy enough to want to find out what's happening. Are you going to tell me?"

"Ummmm, I might. At the proper time and place."

"Name it!"

"I might have lunch with you at Clifton's downtown."

"Okay. I'll be there," he told her.

"I might be, too."

"*What?*"

"I just said I *might* have lunch with you, remember?"

The click in the receiver was dull and final.

Reid blasted out his breath in a gigantic exhalation. Threatening phone calls, spying on him, threats, accusations. He didn't have to put up with it. He paid taxes—plenty of 'em. He was going to get action on this!

Furiously, he stabbed his finger at the dial, spinning the number of police headquarters.

He hung up.

No, that wouldn't get enough action. He would go see somebody on the force immediately. Somebody...why not Lieutenant Oslow? Yeah, why not?

He didn't have to put up with this. He was innocent, entirely innocent.

Flipping back the covers, Reid sent the strangled cat flopping leadenly to the carpet.

* * *

"I hope you don't mind the smell of fresh paint," Lieutenant Oslow said.

Reid sniffed. "Don't worry. I've smelled worse things in my life."

"Really? Wouldn't think it to look at you. Won't you sit down?"

"If the chair's; not painted."

"It isn't."

Reid sat down.

"Varnished," Oslow said.

The lieutenant held up his hands. "Just a little joke."

"Very," Reid said. "You shouldn't try to be whimsical; it doesn't fit on you. I'm here on serious business."

The policeman seated himself behind his desk.

"This isn't usually good advice in my business, but—shoot."

"I had another weird telephone call."

Oslow nodded. "I understood you were getting them all the time. Why not have your number changed?"

"Why not catch the people making these calls?" the writer demanded.

Oslow leaned back and studied Reid. "Do these people talk to you long?"

"This—this woman this morning had quite a bit to say."

"Well, if you can hold her on the line five minutes, the telephone company can trace it at our request."

"You mean you'll trace every call I receive?"

The detective threw up his hands. "Impossible! The telephone company needs three or four men to check out all the relays. They'd be occupied full time with you. Who's going to pay their salaries? No you'd have to have a man from the department monitor all your calls and check out the threatening ones."

"Look here, I don't want some cop listening to every call I make," Reid pointed out.

"We don't have everything just the way we like it, Mr. Reid. Case in point: you would probably prefer not to receive the anonymous calls at all. But if you want to stop them, you're going to have to have a monitor."

"That's out," Reid said flatly.

Reid hesitated. He had planned to tell Oslow about the meeting he had set up with the woman who had called him, in order to get the police to pick her up. But would they be interested? Could they spare a man? More likely, from Oslow's attitude, they would just tell him that the woman probably wouldn't show up at all, and everybody's time would be wasted.

More important, he was already suspected of strange behavior. If he told of strangling a cat in his bedroom, might he not go on the list of sex perverts? He could just see himself dragged in every time a child was molested, and sooner or later, some hysterical mother was sure to point him out.

Oslow seemed to sense some of the hostility and fear Reid was feeling for the police.

"Look here, Mr. Reid, we want to help you, but you've got to help *us* to help you. You can't be so secretive, trying to cover up things, if you *really* are being bothered by these cultists and need our help to stop them."

Reid stood up. "Maybe I don't need your help. Sorry for taking up your valuable time. Good day."

*   *   *

Clifton's for lunch.
She might show up, huh? Good enough.

Reid stood in line with his tray and received the manufactured portions of food. When he had marched long enough for the food to pile high enough, he passed by the goldfish slithering in their troughs and climbed the stairs to a tiered plateau.

There were blue lights, green plants, white tablecloths—and rushing, elbowing people. It was an, esthetically pleasing madhouse.

He took a table, unloaded his tray, as the white-jacketed boy waited to pounce on it like an owl after a field mouse. Well, he got it. That should make him happy.

Now to wait and watch. And, oh yes, eat.

But who to watch for?

Reid had a pretty good idea, he thought. Doris MacNiter, the girl with the incriminating photograph of him and her sister. That was, of course, if anybody showed up at all.

He had taken a table on the rail, overlooking the ponds two stories below. Down there, he could see dozens of people coming in, going out…

For a second, he stood up to get a better look.

In that second, some force struck him in the small of his back and he pitched forward, toward the tiny fish swimming in a few inches of water two floors below.

*   *   *

Falling.

It was just for an instant, but for that fragment of time he sensed himself falling toward the main floor far below. Then…his hands caught the guardrail and he leaned far out and eased himself back.

He took a deep breath and looked around him. Nobody had noticed how near he had come to falling, perhaps to his death. And what had hit him in the back, almost causing him to fall?

"Jace?"

He turned toward the inquiring female voice.

"Miss…MacNiter?" he said.

The tallish brunet in the tailored dress smiled. "That's right."

"But—you're not Doris. You're—"

"Carla. Carla MacNiter. Who did you think I was, silly?"

Carla. The girl in the photograph. The girl he was supposed to have been beating with a whip.

She didn't look beat. She looked in excellent health, despite Doris' fears about her impending collapse. She seemed very strong indeed, like some jungle leopard girl from a pre-censorship comic book. Her breasts looked like muscles instead of mammary glands. She licked her red chops and smiled at him.

"Aren't you going to invite me to sit down?" Carla asked.

He motioned her to a chair. "Aren't you having anything to eat?"

"We'll see."

Reid sat down and studied her face for a moment.

"What are you after, Miss MacNiter? What was the meaning of that call this morning?"

"You know what it meant," the girl said suddenly, intensely, "and you know I'm not 'Miss MacNiter' to you; I can never be that to you again."

Reid found himself blinking rapidly. "Lady, up to this minute you've never been *anything* to me. Nothing but a voice on the telephone."

"You remember *that*, do you? You at least remember the telephone call."

"I wish to hell I didn't."

"You don't have to be blasphemous in your language," Carla said in a hushed whisper.

Blasphemy—that was taking the name of the deity in vain, not hell. But she was right—his language was getting rough. Then so was his disposition.

"Come on," he said. What were you up to? How could you see into my bedroom?"

"You know the Chosen have eyes that can see everywhere."

"You and Big Brother. But I don't like spying, Miss MacNiter. I consider it an invasion of privacy, one I could take into court."

Carla smiled. "Along with the dead cat?"

He felt his face burn. "My fine from the S. P. C. A. would be less than yours for extortion."

"What have I tried to extort from you?" Carla asked, lowering her eyes. "Perhaps I am trying to force you to surrender your fair white body to me?"

"Lady, there are some strange characters in this town, male and female. I don't know what the devil, you're after."

"Don't you? Don't you know what the devil?"

"That's what I'm here to find out!" he stormed.

"You won't find out here," she said. "You can learn the rest if you meet me at Ocean View Park at eight tonight."

"Why should I meet you there?" he demanded.

Her eyes became level on his. "Why did you meet me here?"

Then she stood up and stepped in with a party of four moving down the aisle.

She couldn't do this to him, show up for a few moments, tantalize him and disappear.

He left his food untouched and hurried down the isle after her, but already she was lost in the crush of humanity.

Then Reid saw her for a second more, a second of midnight hair in the serpent of a crowd rippling down the stairs.

Pushing, shoving, kneading, he parted the ranks to make way for his body. Once he thought he saw her on the steps.

And once again, there was some unseen force striking him in the back and he was falling.

His knee struck the step painfully and he stopped falling. He looked around him swiftly at other legs and knees and shoes—men, women and children. A man with a built-up heel, a woman with very thick legs.

Hands were helping him up from behind.

"You shouldn't run on the steps," a hoarse voice advised him. "It can be dangerous."

And the hands and the voice were lost in the crowd.

Yes, Reid thought, sweat stinging his forehead, this could be dangerous.

He would be a fool to go out to the pier tonight—a complete fool.

But the big problem was how he was going to be able to wait until that time.

*　　　*　　　*

He parked the car and looked out at the twin Ferris wheels orbiting through the star-pointed sky.

The music of the amusement park drifted through the air like an aroma of browning sugar. The salt-mist of the nearby sea complicated the strain.

Reid turned the ignition key free and pocketed it. He climbed out of the car, locked it, and took his bearings.

He hadn't been out here for ten years, but he remembered the pier should be off over there.

He started walking.

This day had been almost unbearable; waiting for the night.

That phone call had been a lousy, way to start the day.

How could she possibly have known he had just killed the kitten?

Could she have planted the damned thing in his bed, placed his hands around it while he slept? No, he couldn't buy that. The dream, the way he woke up, he knew he really had killed the cat. But how could the girl on the telephone know about it so fast?

Well, that was what he had come to Ocean View Park to find out.

This is where she had told him to come, to be on the pier at exactly eight o'clock.

He had waited all day, not keeping appointments, not answering the phone, and he had come, just as she said.

He might not have come if the woman on the phone hadn't given her name—Carla MacNiter.

Doris' sister, the one he was supposed to lash into an orgiastic frenzy with a bullwhip.

He was going to get to the bottom of all of this.

Just then, a volley of shots came from Reid's left.

Of course, he realized—the shooting gallery.

There didn't seem to be really a tremendous number of people in this part of the park. He made his way onto the pier without difficulty and found himself alone. A few small boats were tied up, but there was no activity.

He went out to the end of the pier and looked at the silver trail the moon left on the ocean.

She had promised to be here at eight. It was now seven past eight.

Gunshots seemed to separate themselves from the other sounds of the amusement park. The shooting galleries, of course. But wait. From a shooting gallery, he might hear the bang of the gun, but could he know the sound of the bullet's whine, the wind of its passing?

An irresistible force struck Reid in the back of the head, and he had time to think: Have I come all this way just to find this?

And he fell into a bottomless, swirling darkness, a million years wide.

And the day ended as it had begun—with a dream of Death.

CHAPTER FOUR

"Shot in the back of the head," Inspector Oslow observed.

Sergeant Grubb's two hundred and fifty pound frame shuddered delicately. "The bullet makes such a little hole when it goes in and such a big hole when it comes out."

Oslow turned his collar up against the chill of the morgue. The body lying there on the bottom of the drawer, its skin blue, looked cold. Uncomfortably cold.

"Who would want to kill Reid?" Grubb asked.

"Who knows? A lot of people, I guess. He's been hanging about with some of these weirdos in the cults. Stepped on a few toes, I guess, and got this for his trouble."

Oslow slid the drawer shut, and he and Grubb went back up the corridor toward the attendant's desk.

"The newspapers are going to be in on this one," Grubb said with mixed emotions.

"That means daily 'results'," Oslow said contemptuously.

"Yeah, Frank, but if we break this, we could swing promotions."

"Yeah," Oslow said. "We could swing."

They nodded to the attendant who nodded back to them and checked them out.

They want into the office. The Press was waiting for them.

Oslow looked at their faces. The reporters were personally interested in this one. Maybe because Reid had been a writer, and a writer was something like a newspaperman. Maybe Reid had even been a reporter at one time. He hadn't had a chance to check too far back on him yet.

"Any clues, lieutenant?" voice called.

Some voice always called that.

"Yes, there is a very significant clue. The killer made one fatal mistake that will bring him to justice beyond the shadow of a doubt." Oslow quieted the uproar. "I am not at liberty to reveal this clue. You wouldn't want to impede us in our capture of the killer, would you?"

The grumbling leveled off. Most of these boys didn't give a damn about impeding the work of the police department, as long as they got their stories, but they seldom put their philosophy into words.

"Lieutenant Osgood, why do you think Reid was killed?" a woman, obviously not a police reporter, asked.

"Did you see that movie he wrote?" the lieutenant asked. "And the name is Oslow."

"A movie called—oh, yes, Lieutenant Oslow. No, but I read the book."

"That's even worse," Oslow assured her. "Reid's favorite subject were sex maniacs. Some of them finally made a subject out of him."

A small man with a smaller mustache became very excited. "Lieutenant, Lieutenant, Pawley, *News of the world*, London. Was the body assaulted?"

"It was," Oslow said, and plowed on through the agitated comments, "with a .22 rifle at close range."

The reporters filed out of the morgue office to phone in or write their stories. Even the woman who wasn't a police reporter.

"She reviews books," Grubb supplied him.

"Wonder how good a job she does herself on her diary."

"Lieutenant, I'm worried about something."

"Yes, Grubb?"

"I'm kind of worried about this clue that is going to show up the killer. What is it?"

"Let's let the killer worry about that, too," Oslow said.

*   *   *

When she opened the door, it was obvious Lisa Tanner had been crying.

"Yes? Oh, I believe we've met before. Lieutenant Oslow, isn't it?"

"Yes, ma'am. This is Sergeant Grubb. You haven't met him before."

"Now I see what I've missed. Won't you two come in?"

The policemen went inside and Lisa closed the door.

Her apartment, Oslow thought, was nicer than Reid's. It showed taste, imagination. Lisa Tanner had worked on it.

"Miss Tanner," the lieutenant said, "you know of Mr. Reid's death. We would like you to give us any information that might be of help to us."

Lisa buried her face in her palms for an instant, then took her hands away. "Do you have any information that can help me? I've tried everything but information."

She ambled over to her well-stocked bar and picked up a glass. "I've tried drinking, but I don't seem to have acquired the knack of being an alcoholic. Not yet. I tried another man. A handsome, brilliant young lawyer. But as hard as I worked at it last night, I couldn't achieve tumescence. And I was so much of a drag, he couldn't even get an—"

"Miss Tanner," Oslow persisted, "don't you want Mr. Reid's killer to be caught?"

"I don't know." Lisa shrugged. "I suppose so. I want—I want—but I can't have that, can I? I want…I want another drink. And yes, I want Jace Reid's killer caught."

Lisa put some ice into her glass and built another drink.

"You don't drink on duty, do you?"

"No, ma'am," Oslow said. "Now about Mr. Reid

"Yes. Well, somebody was trying to blackmail him. Are things like that, what you want to know."

"That's right, Miss Tanner. This blackmail thing may be just what we need to know." Grubb and Oslow exchanged glances; the newspapers might learn to love them yet. "What else can you tell us about this?"

Lisa rubbed her pale forehead with gold nails. "There was a girl who came around to Jace's apartment with dirty pictures. Her name was—I wrote it down—wait—Doris MacNiter. At least, that's what she said her name was. She wanted Jace to leave her sister alone."

"Was the sister's name MacNiter, too?" Sergeant Grubb interjected.

"Yes, sergeant, I believe it was," Lisa said patiently, "Carla MacNiter."

"She could have been married," the sergeant said defensively.

"She wasn't married," Lisa said. "According to Doris, she was some kind of sex pervert—she liked men to beat her."

"She liked men to beat her?" Oslow said excitedly. "Just how did she like it? I mean, did the MacNiter girl go into details, details how her sister liked to be beat?"

"She didn't bother with descriptions. She just showed the photographs. They were pretty dirty. Jace claimed they were faked."

"Don't you believe they were faked?" the lieutenant asked sharply.

"Lieutenant," Lisa said wearily, "I learned about boys a long time ago. They may go to Sunday school, they may keep their clothes clean, and always pay their debts promptly. But when it comes to sex—whatever amuses them in sex, they'll do and do it as often as they possibly can. That's the way men are and you may as well accept it."

"Yes, ma'am. These pictures, they were pictures of Reid beating this girl's sister?"

"Yes."

"What did you say the girl looked like?"

"Nice-looking brunet. Medium-sized. No soars or tattoos I could see."

"Thank you, Miss Tanner. That's all, for right now."

"Are you going to try to find the MacNiter Girl?" Lisa wanted to know. "How could you ever find her in a city this big?"

Sergeant Grubb smiled broadly. "The police have their methods, Miss Tanner."

The two men left the apartment and stopped in the hallway.

"The police have their methods, eh, Grubbs?" Oslow said. "What method do you propose we use to locate Doris MacNiter?"

"I was thinking of the phonebook, Frank."

"Good thinking."

*   *   *

Oslow stabbed the button, and looked up at the front of the suburban bungalow. White, average, frame.

Doris opened the door and her frame was well above average.

Oslow took off his hat, and noticed Grubb failed to do so. The contrast was undoubtedly to his favor.

"Good afternoon, Miss MacNiter," Oslow said. "Is your sister at home?"

"Why don't you leave Carla alone?" Doris demanded. "Go on. Get out of here."

Oslow flashed his credentials. "I'm Lieutenant Oslow. I think Sergeant Grub and I had better step inside."

Doris fell back weakly, and the two policemen entered.

"Do you know Jace Reid?" Oslow asked.

"The writer? He's dead. I read it in the paper."

"Did you know him?"

"No."

"Miss MacNiter, we know you were in his apartment."

"I—I met him once. I didn't really know him."

"What was your visit about Miss MacNiter?" Oslow wanted to know.

"Personal. Private. I won't tell you."

"Was it about a photograph?"

"How did—? I'm not going to say anything more until I see a lawyer."

"You're making our position very difficult," Oslow assured her. "Blackmail is a serious charge. You can go to prison for a great many years for blackmail."

"I wasn't trying to blackmail anybody. I don't know what you are talking about!"

"Take it easy, Frank," Grubb said. "Calm down. You're scaring the girl. Next thing you know you'll be hitting her. You should take it easy."

"I want the truth," the lieutenant said, "and I intend to get it."

"What do you want me to say?" Doris pleaded, her eyes round and moist.

"How long had you known Reid?"

"I only saw him once, at his apartment. It was Carla that—"

"Yes," Oslow filled in the silence. "What about Carla?"

Doris exhaled and dropped her eyes to the floor.

"Carla knew him. He was her boy friend. They were two of a kind. They deserved each other. But…Carla is my sister."

"Where is Carla?"

Doris shook her head. "Not here."

"But where?"

"I don't know. She goes off. I don't know where."

"Miss MacNiter," Grubb said gently, "it will be easier on you if you tell the truth."

Doris laughed shortly. "Oh, I know your little act. I've read about it, seen it in the movies. You, sergeant, are the kind, understanding cop, and the lieutenant is the tough, brutal cop. Between you, I'm supposed to break. A cute little act."

Grubb shook his head sadly. "With Oslow, it's no act, Miss."

"Never mind," Oslow said shortly. "We can find your sister without your help, Miss MacNiter. Come on, sergeant."

The two men left and the girl stood alone in her house.

The telephone.

They wouldn't have had time to have it tapped yet. Of course, they might have done it before they came in.

No, they just couldn't have, because she couldn't go out to a public telephone. Her legs wouldn't hold her up that long.

Doris went to the phone and began dialing.

*　　　*　　　*

Lisa listened to the sound of dialing behind the door. Doris MacNiter was in there. She had just seen the policemen, Oslow and Grubb, pull away from in front. She had Doris all to herself. Tracing her phone had been easy.

She started to open the door but something made her hesitate.

Lisa pressed her mass of red hair against the door panel and listened. She couldn't hear well. Ghosts of words passed through the walls.

"...Afraid...must do something about him..."

"Reid!"

Then a refrigerator started up inside and all the words were lost.

Instinctively, Lisa opened the door.

Doris stared at her standing in the doorway as if she had been caught in the bathroom doing something she shouldn't do.

Doris hung up hastily.

"Who are you? What are you doing here?"

"You remember me well enough, Doris. We met at Jace Reid's apartment," Lisa told her flatly.

"Oh. More about him again. Why don't you all let me alone?"

Lisa moved in closer to the brunet girl. "You came to us, Doris. You came to us with the whole story, and with that photograph."

"I was just trying to protect my sister," Doris said quickly. "You don't have to blame me—"

"Blame you for what, Doris?" Lisa demanded. "What's there to blame you for?"

"Nothing!" Doris screamed. "Jace Reid preyed on my family, forced my sister into the most hideous sex perversions, and you blame me for something!"

"It must be your guilty conscience, Doris—I haven't blamed you for anything *yet.*"

"You stay away from me," the brunet girl told Lisa.

Suddenly, Doris backed off.

"You just stay right there."

"Guilt makes people afraid, I suppose. What have you to feel guilty about?"

"Nothing."

"Doris, let me tell you—Jace Reid was my man. The police have to be easy on you—I don't. If I thought you'd killed Jace, I'd murder you with my bare hands. And if I thought you knew *who* killed Jace, I'd torture you half to death to find that out."

"Don't think those things," Doris said. Her face was pale. Her thrusting breasts were heaving spasmodically. "I don't know *anything.*"

"You know something," Lisa said. "You were talking to somebody on the telephone about Jace. I heard you."

Doris turned very, very pale, making the red of her lip rouge stand out like a vampire's kiss. "That was my girl friend. I was just telling her about the police being here to question me. That's all."

"You're lying," Lisa flung at her. "Don't try lying to another woman, baby. A man might not be able to take his eyes off those breasts of yours but I was looking you in the eye."

Doris had her back to the wall; she had gone as far as she could go. "What I do in my home, who I call, is my own business. Get out of here!"

"A while back, you told me to stay right where I was. Make up your mind."

Lisa moved closed to the frightened brunet girl pressed against the wall.

"You'll tell me, Doris, you'll tell me what you know about the murder of Jace…"

Doris threw her arm out, pushing Lisa aside. But Lisa grabbed the brunet by her dark hair before she could escape and yanked her nearer.

Letting out a short shriek, Doris stamped backwards and brought her high heel down into Lisa's instep. With a short cry, Lisa brought her knee up between Doris' buttocks, and wrapped her arms around the girl's bust.

Doris struggled to free herself from Lisa's grasp, mashing her breasts against Lisa's forearms. Reaching over her shoulder, the brunet grabbed some of Lisa's red hair and jerked viciously.

Gritting her teeth, Lisa formed her hands into claws whose nails bit into the soft globes of flesh on Doris' chest. A desperate strength filled Doris and she twisted around until the two girls were facing, each other, locked in each other's arms, their sets of full breasts mashed and nestled together, heaving and indenting with anger-hardened nipples.

Their bodies twisted and pushed at each other until they toppled to the floor, their hose-encased legs tangled.

Lisa felt her hips strike the floor with a painful jar and Doris was on top of her, punching her in the stomach with a small fist again and again.

Red lights flashed in Lisa's mind, easing into black, flashing and easing, flashing and easing…

She knew she had to stop Doris. There was no question whatsoever about letting her keep on doing it to her.

Lisa reached up and grabbed one of Doris' breasts.

She twisted—*hard*. Until Doris screamed and fell back.

When the brunet began to fall, Lisa grabbed her by one nylon-coated thigh and levered her back, until her head cracked against the floor.

Lisa straddled her, grabbed the younger girl by the ears and began to beat her head against the carpet.

"No use!" Doris gasped. "You can't get Reid back!"

The words cut like a knife, through her hysteria, and Lisa was left feeling sick and weak and helpless. She pitched off Doris, onto her own hands and knees.

"You can't get Reid back!" Doris cried, sobbing and jeering.

Lisa got to her feet and stumbled toward the door.

"You can't get him back, whatever you do to me, or yourself!"

The air of day bit Lisa in the face, and with it full realization—Jace was dead.

Jace was dead.

Dead.

CHAPTER FIVE

He couldn't believe the headline he was reading.

It was a small headline on an inside page, but it said: JACE REID, 'SEX FIEND' WRITER FOUND MURDERED.

He didn't believe a word of it. The story was false from start to finish.

He should know. He was Jace Reid.

Reid flung the newspaper off the bed and set the coffee cup on the nightstand.

He started to get out of bed, and then discovered that they hadn't removed the restraint.

*   *   *

"The corpse doesn't have any fingerprints," Grubb told Oslow.

Oslow took a swig from his paper container of coffee and set it down on his scarred, ringed desk. "That's odd," he said.

"Yeah."

"Reid wasn't a professional criminal. You lots of times find small-time hoods who have skin grafts or acid burns to take off the prints. How were Reid's erased?"

"The M. E. couldn't tell yet. Just like they just— vanished."

Oslow rubbed his chin speculatively. "Reid must have had quite a past. Something he felt he really had to cover up."

"What's your guess?"

Oslow shrugged. "Rape, maybe. Or Statutory. Child molesting. Something to do with sex. People try to cover up sex crimes more than any other, except maybe embezzling."

"We can't find the MacNiter girl's sister," Grubb went on consulting his notes. "Talked to some of her employers on the phone. Hard worker. Strange girl, though. That's what they said—strange. Unemployment has no record of her at this time. She's dropped out of sight."

"Huggins and Keen are staking Dons today?"

"Yeah."

"Doris will lead us to Carla, sooner or later," Oslow said confidently.

*　　*　　*

Jacc Reid finished loosening the straps around his legs.

He had a dim memory of somebody loosening the one around his chest, and leaving him with a breakfast tray, complete with morning newspaper.

He felt—odd. Mopey. No, *dopey*. He had been drugged.

Was this what success meant in Hollywood? Being hounded and even attacked by a bunch of crackpots? He would have been better off staying in New York and writing for the few remaining pulp magazines. Would success spoil Jace Reid? If he believed the papers, it had not only spoiled him—it had killed him.

No, I'm not dead. Don't think crazy. But you feel so strange—maybe this is what it feels like to be dead?

That's just the dope talking. You aren't dead. Corpses don't eat breakfast.

Reid got to his feet. Funny, the room had seemed small while he was lying in bed, but now that he was standing, it seemed big. *Big.* Big as Grand Central Station.

The bigness of it smothered him and he sank to his knees.

The tip of his nose almost touched the newspaper lying on the bed.

Jace Reid, 32, nationally known author of mystery and horror stories, was found dead today, his body floating in the waters off Santa Monica. He had been shot through the head with a medium-caliber bullet at such an angle to make suicide unlikely or impossible...

Who was that corpse, if it isn't me?

"The body they found *was* you," a voice said as if in answer to his thoughts.

"That's crazy," Reid said uncertainly. "I'm alive, I'm here. But where are you, Voice?"

Reid realized his senses weren't sharp enough to tell where the voice was coming from. It might be a concealed electronic speaker, or maybe somebody was just outside the door talking through the keyhole.

No, no, Reid thought, you *look* through a keyhole, not talk through one. That's how he knew I was looking at the newspaper...

"You are here, Jace Reid," the Voice said, "but *how do you know you're alive?*"

"I think, therefore I am."

That Voice. He had heard it before. Of course! It was the voice on the telephone. Disguised, obviously. Weird.

"I know you," Reid managed, bracing his hands on the cotton-soft bed. "You're some kind of dirty sex pervert. You called me on the phone. Sex pervert."

"Of course. I don't deny it. There's nothing I like better than a nice ripe pair of baloozas. I am a sex pervert. But then, so are you."

"No. No."

"How can you write so feelingly about sex perverts then if you aren't one?"

"Write about murderers, too. But I'm not one."

"No. You'd just like to be. And don't worry. You soon will be a murderer. The very best kind of murderer."

"No," Reid protested weakly.

"Think, Jace Reid—*think*. You're dead. You're a sex pervert. Soon you'll be a murderer. Doesn't that mean anything to you?"

"No." He couldn't think of anything else to say.

"You *must* understand. You are a *vampire.*"

"Crazy, crazy."

"I know. All the silly superstitions. The bad horror movies. But vampires exist. There is much truth to the old legends."

"Vampires are dead," Reid reasoned doggedly. "I'm not dead."

"But you are dead. You know very well they found your body floating in the ocean."

"Shouldn't find my body," Reid persisted. "Should come back to life."

"You have. Energy projection. You don't think a vampire lives for centuries in the same moldy piece of clay? Astral projection. Very scientific. Dr. Rhine at Duke

134

University is conducting experiments along these lines. You aren't quite accustomed to your new astral body yet."

"You say I'm a spirit, and I'm still interested in sex?"

"Well, aren't you? Think of the old legends. Do you think vampires sneak into the bedrooms of gorgeous blondes just for blood alone?"

"If we're spirits, why do we need blood?" Reid inquired out of some growing curiosity.

"Not actually blood. Life force. You've always had the makings of a vampire. All your life you've been drawing off the life-force of people—your parents who supported you while you were getting started writing and who went to an early grave, your agent, Lisa Tanner, whom you've used in every possible way—"

"Liar!" Reid screamed. "Dirty foul-mouthed liar!"

"—And you became ever greedier. You had to have *all* the life-force of that innocent kitten, and soon—soon—"

Reid beat on the door with both fists now sure the Voice was just outside.

After he beat on the door for a long time, it opened.

In walked a giant.

A one-eyed giant.

CHAPTER SIX

"That isn't Jace Reid!" Lisa cried out. The sound was dismally as triumphant as a Beethoven symphony.

"Are you sure?" Grubb asked sympathetically. "There isn't much face left to identify."

Lisa stared and stared at the body on the slab to reassure herself. "That is *not* Jace."

"Miss Tanner," Lieutenant Oslow said, "death changes a body. All the little things you knew in a person leave when they die. The expression, the posture, the being goes and leaves a strange hulk you think you must never have known. But the hulk is all that is left. That's all there is to identify when the identity is gone."

"I knew Jace Reid's body, Lieutenant. *Intimately.* There are some things death can't erase. Marks that living makes on a man. This man doesn't have those marks. He looks like Jace. But that isn't his body."

The attendant closed the drawer at Oslow's signal.

"Thank you for your cooperation, Miss Turner," Oslow said.

"You're through with me? I can go?"

"I'll have Sergeant Grubb drive you home, if you like."

"I'll forego that pleasure. Good-day."

The tall redhead, striking in an incredibly well tailored black suit, turned briskly and click-clacked down the vacant corridor of the morgue. The three men watched with appreciation the movements of her hips as she left. The silence was almost reverent.

"Think she's right about it not being Reid, Frank?" Grubb asked finally.

"Yes, I do. But I may be wrong. I don't think she's lying—not even to herself. She's a pretty level-headed cookie."

"Then where do we go from here?"

"After the real Reid," Oslow said. "Somebody wanted us to think this was Reid. He looks like him. He had his billfold, clothes and jewelry."

"And he didn't have no fingerprints."

"Somebody was thorough. Like they were used to planning murder. At least on paper."

"Reid?" Grubb asked. "You think Reid killed this man and tried to make it look like it was him?"

Oslow shrugged. "Men have tried to disappear before. He lit up a cigarette. "Not many of them make it."

The attendant was still staring down the long corridor. He rubbed the white stubble around his lips. "She was a nice one. Kind of like to see her here with nothing on but a sheet."

Oslow threw his new cigarette down and ground it out like a snake.

"You won't get to see her that way."

The attendant grinned. "Yes, I will. Sooner or later they all come here."

"It'll be later," Oslow said. "Much too late for you old man."

"You're just jealous," the attendant said peevishly.

The creature in the white jacket was seven feet tall—six eight or ten—and it wore a pair of glasses with one lens completely black. The effect was piratical.

"What do you want to go banging on the door like that for?" the one-eyed giant asked Reid, the voice deep and rasping.

Only, he realized with a numb wave of incredulity, that it wasn't a giant, but a *giantess*. The reddish brown hair was chopped, rather than cut, short, and all the bulges under the tunic weren't muscles. This was a woman, a square block of female flesh. But he corrected himself again. She wasn't really female. She was sexless. He couldn't believe she was interested in sex with *anybody*.

His effort at reasoning the real nature of this apparition left him weak. He didn't want to have to think anymore. But something nagged at his brain.

"The Voice," he said. "Voice outside my door."

"Hearing voices, huh? I know what you want. I got what you want."

Reid doubted that. He doubted it even more as the huge form drew nearer, nearer, and reached out for him. Finally,

Reid saw the silver hypodermic in her hand. *"This is* what you want."

He shook his head and took a step backward.

"Don't want it, huh? Well, you will. In a few weeks—days even—you'll want it worse than you ever wanted anything in your life. How you're going to want this needle, you don't know. And you'll have to pay. Barrie's got the needle for you here, but you'll have to pay her. You get her money from home and pay for your nice needles. Else you don't get 'em. But right now, you can have all you want. Isn't that nice of Barrie? She's going to shoot you so full of happy stuff it'll be coming out of your ears."

Reid took a further step backwards and everything began to spin as he fell onto the bed.

"Here's your nice needle, Mr. Raft."

"Wait a minute," Reid protested indignantly, "my name's not Raft."

"That's what your voices tell you, huh?" Barry said, holding the hypodermic up to the light.

"My name's Jace Reid. See. Here, look. My picture's in the newspaper."

"That says Jace Reid is dead, Mr. Raft."

"A mistake. A mistake, I tell you. I'm Reid. Not Raft—*Reid!*"

"Sure, Mr. Reid. Hold your arm steady now."

A banana-bunch of fingers came out and seized Reid's arm. The sheer mass of the woman was overwhelming. He felt as small and weak as an infant. It was not only useless to struggle against her, he felt, but self-demeaningly silly.

The needle grew at him as the probe of a spaceship in a science fiction movie.

He watched as the tip punctured his skin, and the thumb, thick as a child's wrist, pushed the colorless liquid into him. So far, he was only being joypopped in the skin, not mainlined in a vein. Or perhaps it was too much trouble for Barrie to find the vein just now, with him conscious and struggling. Main lining, probably could wait until later, when he was unconscious or anxious to get the shot.

"Get a nice sleep now," Barrie advised him briefly, and went out the door, closing and locking it behind her.

As soon as the door closed, Reid dashed the coffee cup down on the floor, shattering it into as many fragments as an unsuccessful I. C. B. M. He picked up a piece and slashed his arm open with it.

"Better quiet down in there now, Mr. Raft, or I'll just have to come back in and strap you down nice and tight again," Barrie assured him warmly through the door.

So I'm a vampire? Reid thought.

He sucked the blood from the open wound of his arm, finding the iron taste not unpleasant. The blood not only looked like tomato juice, it tasted the same way.

Reid spat the blood out, sucked some more, and spat it out.

There was a small pool of saliva, interlaced with red fibers, beside the bed.

Reid tore off a strip from the bottom of his nightgown and wrapped it around his arm. It soaked through almost immediately.

Now, he thought, now all I can do is wait and see.

The room curved in on him and he floated down into a delicious softness.

He knew he was falling asleep and he wondered if he had done enough, he wondered if he would ever wake up.

CHAPTER SEVEN

Jace Reid woke up slowly.

His body was tossed casually on the bed, half under the covers, half on top.

He hadn't been strapped down and no one was in sight. His head was clear.

It had worked.

He had drawn off enough of the narcotic like so much snake venom so that he had come out of it much sooner then *they* had expected.

His arm was clotted and dried. Good. He hadn't bled to death. Missed the artery.

There was an insidious crawling ache throughout his body that he supposed was a withdrawal symptom from the dope. But he hadn't been on the stuff long enough for it to be serious, and a craving for it would be only physical, not psychological, with him.

Reid labored out of bed. He was weak but he could see— and think—straight.

A weapon. He needed a weapon to bash Barrie's brains out when she finally returned.

The breakfast tray on the nightstand hadn't been touched. The tray itself was light plastic, and the silverware lighter plastic. The dishes were thick restaurant china. He might try breaking one and use a large fragment to slit Barry's throat. But the plan seemed impractical. The plate itself wasn't heavy enough to even dent the giantess' thick cranium.

The nightstand—bolted securely to the floor he discovered.

For the first time, he went to the window.

On the inside was a heavy wire mesh in front of the glass. A metal awning kept the sunlight from coming directly into the room. In the distance, he could see the giant letters on the slope spelling out HOLLYWOOD. From this, he decided he was probably in one of the sanitariums in the heart of the city, between Vermont and Alvarado.

He crossed over to the door. It didn't even jar under his shoulder.

Reid paced back and forth.

He glanced at the window.

Sunlight.

Then he couldn't be a vampire or he would be dead if he was outside his grave during the day!

He shook his head. That was crazy. That had all been while he was under the dope. It probably hadn't been real at all, only a dream.

But Barrie and her needle was no dream. She would be back soon and give him another shot.

Pretty soon Reid wouldn't care who was keeping him here or why; he would just wait impatiently for Barrie to come and give him his fix.

Even that wouldn't be so nice, because Barrie was a sadist.

Much of the times she would probably withhold the shots to watch Reid wretch in the agony of withdrawal.

No, it wouldn't be a pleasant life and no one would ever look for him because everyone thought he was dead.

What happened to him the rest of his life depended on what he did in the next few minutes.

Of course…Reid thought. There was an old, old way to slay the giant.

He tossed the bedclothes aside and peeled off the pillowcase. Into it he shoved all the dishes from the tray, the broken fragments of the coffee cup. He twisted the pillowcase until the dishes made a lump at the bottom.

He stood for a long time behind the door with the sweat running down his temples.

He gave up.

He stood there only because he didn't want to make a fool of himself, to be trapped and later on to have to say to himself he could have avoided it if he had only stood there a few more minutes.

There was a fumbling at the lock.

Reid began whirling the pillowcase around and around above his head.

The door inched open.

Barrie was cautiously looking in.

The bedclothes, Reid realized. He should have made a dummy with them. He had seen it often enough in the movies. But strangely enough, when he had tossed the blankets about he had accidently sculpted what might be taken for a sleeping man.

The Whirr of the loaded pillowcase was a retreating and approaching insect above Reid's head. Barrie's great bulk slipped into the room.

Reid swung the weight around once more and let the sling go. It struck the giant in the center of the forehead, dissolving her slow expression of surprise, and Barrie fell.

The big woman sank majestically to her knees, she swayed precariously for a moment, then righted herself. Slowly, one foot at a time, she got to her feet.

"I'm going to have to punish you severely for that," she told Reid.

The sling lay, a pile of useless trash, across the room from Reid. He had no weapons. Everything in the room was bolted down to protect it and him from his alleged madness.

Barrie clawed out one hand to secure Reid's nightshirt, to steady Reid's body for the blows she was going to let rain on it.

Reid led with his right with all he had. Literally, all he had. This was it. One sucker punch. It wasn't much.

It was enough.

Barrie's head snapped back and her body followed it. She lay spread-eagle on her back, out cold.

He rubbed at the satisfying pain in his right hand. Of course, he couldn't possibly have knocked the giant out if she hadn't been just barely conscious after being hit in the head with the loaded sling, but still, it was…satisfying…to do it this way.

Now, there was something he had to do.

Reid reached down and unzipped Barrie's pants.

She was wearing *man's* pants, he noticed. Just what he needed.

CHAPTER EIGHT

Reid made his way carefully along the hallways of the old house. The place was completely strange; he hadn't the least idea where he was going or what he might find. All he could see was a repetition of closed and locked doors painted dark brown and walls stained light brown.

The stairs, at last.

He went down cautiously, hitching up the pants he was wearing. Strangely, Barrie's pants almost fit him. The giant was all torso. Reid hadn't bothered with the attendant's tent of a shirt. The top of the short-sleeved nightgown he wore looked almost like a sport shirt.

Again, he wished for some kind of a weapon.

He regretted having used the syringe on Barrie to keep her knocked out. He should have satisfied himself with locking her in and taking the hypo with him. Even the empty case would have been some help with its needle. That would do some damage. He didn't know what he might run into.

The sudden sound shocked through him.

Laughter.

A wash of laughter against the sea of shadows that pooled at the bottom of the steps.

Reid waded in.

Light spilled out clearly from an open door to the left.

The laughter led him to the door and burst upon him.

An old man was inside chuckling with a woman.

Reid watched through the crack left by the open door between it and its hinge-board.

Both of them were in white, seemingly a doctor and a nurse. The man was old to the point of feebleness. His head was almost bald except for the few spears of reddish-brown hair that toned down the sheen of taut skin. The woman was forty, broad of beam, still handsome. Both of them were giggling.

"You know it," the doctor said. "You know, Miss Edmonds, that we shouldn't laugh at the patients. They're sick people. Still, when she actually put it on her head for a hat."

Reid frowned. Could that be the Voice he heard, first on the phone, then outside his cell door? It could be, but then that Voice could be anybody, even a dream.

"Yes," the nurse giggled, "I remember, Doctor Inge."

Reid stepped into the room.

Inge turned around, his upper lip working. "Who are you?"

"I'm not anybody named 'Raft'."

"A patient! A *patient*. Barrie! Oh, *Barrie!*"

Reid shook his head. "She won't be coming. She's in my cell, strapped down, shot up to the ears with dope from her own needle."

"Cell? Cell? What are you talking about, young man? This is Dr. Inge's Home for the Nervous. Right, Miss Edmonds?"

Miss Edmonds swallowed and nodded mutely.

"Nervous Nervous like hopheads and alcoholics? I'm neither. How did I get here? Who put me here?"

"I…don't have that information available…"

"WHO?"

Inge winced. "Mrs. Raft, of course. She committed you while Barrie was on duty. She signed the papers. It's all legal!"

A senseless fury took hold of Reid and moved him forward, raising his hand.

Inge scampered around behind his desk and clawed open a drawer. He pulled out a gun and pointed it at him.

"No further," Inge warned. "No further—or I'll use restraint. Miss Edmonds, telephone the police."

Cautiously, facing Reid all the time, Miss Edmonds inched toward the desk, and the white telephone on it.

"You don't want to call the police," Reid said. "You know you don't want to do that. I've seen enough of your little operation to know that. Which way is out?"

Inge wet his lips. "You aren't leaving, Mr. Raft. Oh my, no, we couldn't allow that. Not for anything." The gun became steadier in the old man's hand. "Turn around. Back up the stairs. You're going back. You have to."

"No, I don't," Reid said steadily. "I won't. Not for anything."

The gun wavered in Dr. Inge's hand. Then became steady. It raised slightly. It became very steady. Very steady and very black with a large round hole at the end of the barrel.

"Let him leave," a woman's voice commanded.

The girl stood in the doorway in a black dress, belted with glistening patent leather. Her eyes were dark as her hair.

"No," Inge whined. "He can't go. He *can't.*"

"Can't he?" the girl sneered.

With a single motion, she unclasped her belt and struck the old man across the face with it. He dropped the gun and pressed his palms across the bridge of his nose.

"My eyes! Miss Edmonds, see to my eyes! Immediately!"

As the nurse fearfully rushed to the old man's aid the girl smiled and flipped the free end of the belt up in the air and caught it.

"Come on with me, Jace Reid. My car's outside."

It was. A black hardtop convertible in the luxury class.

The girl drove and he sat watching her for a moment, and the tall palms lining the middle-class residential streets.

"I know you, don't I?" Reid asked finally. "You're Doris MacNiter."

"No," the girl said. "I'm Clara MacNiter."

CHAPTER NINE

"This is my place," Carla said softly in the billowing darkness. "What do you think of it?"

"It's dark," Reid said.

"Yes."

He fumbled for a light switch beside the door. Of course a girl like this might light by candles or whale oil, but—the lights went on.

Reid blinked.

This wasn't a woman's place. It was a man's, he was sure. Decorated like a hunting lodge, it sported guns and knives and whips on the wood-paneled walls. On the mantel above the fireplace was even a small, mounted wild animal of the cat family. Wildcat, bobcat... He shook his head.

"Who's here?" he demanded. "You brought me here to meet somebody, didn't you? This isn't *your* apartment."

"Yes, it is. All mine. I've spent a lot on decorating it. Do you like it?"

"Yes," he said, *"I* like it. Maybe not to live in all the time, but to go up to the North woods and stay in for a couple of weeks once a year."

"I'm glad you like it, Jace," Carla said. "I tried to fix it up nice for you when you come here. I know you'll like this place much better than my room over at Doris' place."

"Just a minute! More of that line. I've never seen you before tonight, and I only saw your sister that once."

"I know. I'm sorry about that. She had no business trying to interfere." Carla moistened her lips. "Do you want to do it now?"

Carla unclasped her belt from her dress.

Reid shut his eyes hard and tried to think.

It was no use.

He couldn't think. It was like trying to write that story the editor wanted; and staring at the white sheet of paper in the typewriter until you went snow blind. The new *Playboy* or *Galaxy* or *Showcase* lay on your desk, and finally, it was much easier to not bother trying to think, but to build yourself a drink and pick up a magazine.

"Why don't you take the rest off?" he asked out of some subconscious curiosity.

Silently, Clara slipped the dress over her head and let it run into a foam of fabric.

He looked at her body, naked except for the euphemisms of black nylon lace. Now he knew why she had the feline wild animal mounted above the fireplace. It complimented and echoed her body. Her breasts were full-blown and whistle-worthy, her legs' strong curves led to rich promise, but he couldn't take his eyes off her stomach. Her stomach and its navel-dimpled tier of controlled muscles.

"My belt's a nice piece of leather," Carla said huskily, "or there's the new whips over there…" Her finger stabbed out, indicating various coiled snakes on the floor, on the walls, all about the room.

The door's right over there, Reid told himself. But the woman was closer.

Reid stepped forward and grabbed her shoulders. Hard. "I'm not going to…*whip* you."

"No, no," she said softly, twisting her head aside. "We've never done that. You know that is *evil,* wicked. Now you've made me want to do it too. We must be *punished* for that. The whip. The *whip!*"

Her eyes steadied on his, and her white teeth came out to indent her plum of a lower lip.

Okay, he thought. Okay. The answer to all his problems was simple. He was in Hollywood. Everybody in Hollywood was crazy. The trick was not to doubt it or think about it, but just to take it for granted. Everybody in Hollywood was crazy.

The idea of striking a woman repulsed him. It violated his most personal concept of self-respect. But now, he thought feverishly, he was in the country of the mad and he must act accordingly.

He slapped her across the face with the palm of his right hand, and then brought it over backhanded, his knuckles jarring her jaw open.

Carla staggered back and grabbed her face.

"No, you silly fool!" she screamed, seizing his hand, "not *that* way. You'll get my face all marked up."

He disengaged her hand and struck her across the face once again.

Carla blinked, and rubbed her bleeding mouth. "I told you not to do that."

"I don't do everything women tell me to do," he said.

He scooped her up into his arms, and carried her towards the door.

He kicked the door open, and heard the smash as the knob knocked a cavity into the wall plaster.

Carla bounced once when he threw her onto the bed.

He stood a moment, feeling the cool night air of the room slip around him like a cloak.

"What are you waiting for?" Carla whispered. "You might as well get it over with. You might...as well. You might as well!"

Her hips lifted from the bed towards him.

NO, he thought.

This was too unclean. He had known intimacy from a real woman. They had had enough respect for each other that force or domination had not been required. And they had been lucky enough to find pleasure in pleasure itself, not in pain and destruction. By his definition of the word, these things were perforce, *evil*.

Reid stepped away from the bed.

Carla looked up at him, her eyes uncertain, then sure, almost against her will.

"You aren't Jace Reid!" Carla shouted. "You *know* you aren't Jace Reid. You look like him, you talk like him, but—why do you pretend now? You're somebody else! Yes. Or *something* else." Her lips repeated the last words *sotto voce*. "Oh, no. It's really true. You have come back. You've *gone over*. You've become a—but not me! There are so many others. I'd help you get them. But not me! Not me, not—"

He wrestled her back down on the bed, hesitated a moment, then responding to some irresistible stimulus, he sank his teeth into her throat.

Lieutenant Frank Oslow stared at what he had his hands on, he stared at *Doris MacNiter,* and then freeing one hand he picked up the knife and working quickly and savagely he slit and ripped.

Oslow shook his head in puzzlement.

Again, he looked at the name, *Doris MacNiter,* in the corner of the envelope. He put the letter-opener back on his desk and fished in the slit-open end of the letter, and pulled out a sheet of paper.

What could she be writing to the police about?

Oslow snapped the letter open with a flick of his wrist and held it, slightly creased by his thumb.

Lieutenant Oslow:

I have a free moment to write you this. It can not go on any longer, I can see.

I will tell you where Carla is at. She is responsible for monstrously evil things, including, what happened to Jace Reid.

I know now that Carla is an evil force that must be destroyed.

Doris MacNiter

Oslow leaned back. If she were going to tell him where Carla was, why didn't she in this note itself?

Of course, he wanted to find Carla. He felt that she could lead him to Jace Reid, the real Reid, not the body in the morgue.

Grubb was out to dinner.

Oslow reached for his hat.

He would see Doris alone. Yes, he had wanted to see her alone for some time.

Reid looked down at the still form of the girl, her naked body bluish white in the moonlight that spilled in through the window.

She was still, he thought, still as the dead. He had finished with her, and this is how he had left her.

Carla turned her head towards him, her eyes closed, and smiled, showing twin rows of sharp, white teeth glittering with green pearls in the filtered light.

None of it made sense. None of it.

Least of all Carla's accusation that he wasn't Jace Reid. Or that he was, as if he shouldn't be. Or that he had come back, or that he had not come back. Mad!

But did he have room to talk? he accused himself. Why had he gnawed at her throat that way. A momentary sexual passion, or was it that he was testing the accusation that he was a vampire, no more mad than some of the rest of the things that had happened to him. If so, he had flunked the test. Like most people, his teeth weren't sharp enough or strong enough to break the skin.

She had fainted then. That had been her most normal reaction since he had first met her. He had wanted to leave, but not to have her follow him or alert the police. In the bathroom, he had looked for a towel, and found a bottle of powerful prescription sleeping pills. As she had started to rouse, he had pressed two tablets on her and in minutes she had sunk back into sleep.

There was no time for him to sleep.

Why had it happened to him? The accusations, the suspicions, the threats, the blackmail, the lure to the pier and the attack, waking up in the sanitarium and escaping from it. There had to be a reason behind the elaborate nightmare in which he found himself. A logical, mundane, everyday kind of motive. Love, hate, revenge, money, politics.

It was no use.

He couldn't solve the problem anymore than Aristotle could fathom the nature of the universe by simply sitting and thinking about it. It needed going out, finding out.

But I can't do anything, he reminded himself, I'm still dead.

How did a man start to live again?

Go to the police, the newspapers? Where did you start?

Lisa.

Lisa should know first. She had the right as his agent, and his—whatever she was to him.

He looked over to the telephone. Maybe the shock wouldn't be so great…but he knew that it would. If he were there, it might be easier on her.

Leaving the bedroom, he went into the darkened living room.

The stuffed cat on the mantel looked as if it were going to leap on him and devour his vitals.

But it didn't.

CHAPTER TEN

Lisa Turner sat under the soft veil of smoke-colored twilight, broken by the pendulum of a neon dawn beating in every second from the nightclub across the court.

The desk lamp was a silver dollar of light in the agnostic's hell of dreamless black on the offbeat.

She was writing words on paper with a fountain pen and reading them to herself as she leaned forward, her amber hair spilling across her cheek like the aftermath of a wild animal's love pat in its red rivulets.

Reid entered quietly, using his key that was hidden in their special place near the door.

The drizzle of words fell on his hearing like the first suggestion of summer rain in a field of violets.

"…When a writer brings hope to the human heart, he is called 'inspired'. When he touches your naked soul with the claws of horror, he is called 'posesses'. The works of Jace Reid are both 'inspired' and 'possessed'. Inspired by agencies as old as sin, and possessed by forces as new as the Secret Police of any shiny new totalitarian empire. But he has given us not only horror, but hope as well. He has given us a hope for horror; a willingness to believe that we will at least stay alive long enough to experience the new horrors that life undoubtedly holds in store for us…"

"Lisa, I'm not dead," Reid said softly. "It was a mistake."

As if she didn't see or hear the taller shadow standing among other shadows, Lisa read on:

"…He has built monuments out of the black, turgid stuff that coagulates and pulses in the obscure corners of the human spirit, building materials untouched by tidier craftsmen, clean of art…"

"Lisa!" he said sharply. "You don't need to write that now. I won't be needing an obituary."

"Yes, you will," Lisa said, rising, her voice and face running out of shape, "because…because…I'm going to kill you myself, with my bare—" She covered her face and cried.

It was the first time he had ever seen her cry, and he took her into his arms clumsily.

"Why," Lisa demanded over their tall glasses of strong drink, "*why* didn't you warn me, why didn't you get in touch with me after the story broke?"

"I…was in a hospital," he said euphemistically. There was no point going into a long and lurid story at the moment. "Time's vitally important, Lisa. You remember that girl with the photographs. Doris MacNiter. I've got to get in touch with her. Tomorrow, I want you to go out and hire a private detective to locate her for me."

"I've already located her," Lisa said flatly.

"How? Did she come back or call?"

"No," she said. "I called. I called all the MacNiter's in the phonebook, asking for Doris until I recognized her voice. I have the address."

"Let me have it."

"Why?"

"I have to go there right away. There's something I've got to discuss with her."

"Something about the man who was killed? Something about what happened to you? What is it?"

"It's," Reid said, "a family matter."

*　　　*　　　*

A busy night, Reid realized with grim horror.

I leave Carla sleeping in Hollywood, rush to Beverly Hills to see Lisa, now I'm dashing to the Silver Lake area above Sunset to find Doris.

He drove Carla's Volkswagen with uneasy speed on the always-busy streets of Los Angeles.

With the beacon of City Hall winking over his left shoulder, he took one of the fibrous offshoots from Sunset and climbed into the tiered residential area.

He spotted the white block building with the blue lights on it and the number he wanted. 327-½.

He left the car and found the number.

After a few moments of ringing, Doris MacNiter opened the door—and screamed.

Almost without thinking, Reid clamped his hand over the girl's mouth and forced her back inside flinging her down on a couch.

Her eyes were wide with terror.

"If I take my hand away now, will you be quiet?" he asked.

Her eyes stared at him uncomprehendingly for a few seconds, then…slowly, she nodded.

He didn't quite trust her but he eased his hand away.

No scream.

"That's better," he said.

"You're dead," Doris said. "You're dead."

"Come on now, do I look like a ghost?"

"They never look like ghosts. They come in the night and do strange things to me and they never look like ghosts. But they are!"

Reid shook her roughly by the shoulders, causing her head and breasts to bobble.

"Come on. Snap out of it, Kid. I'm a live man. You."

"You're *really* alive?" Doris asked hopefully.

"Count on it."

"Then what are you doing here?"

Reid took a deep breath. That was a good question. He had to start somewhere.

"I want you to tell me all about your sister Carla."

"Oh, no," she moaned. "Oh, no."

"Why not?"

"She'd kill me."

"Okay. You've told me one thing already. Carla's own sister thinks she'd kill her if she talked. But you are going to talk, baby. You've got to talk. I'm going crazy without the answers. *I've got to have them.*"

"What do you want to know?"

"What don't I want to know?" Reid yelled. "I've been kidnapped, beaten up and accused of my own murder. I'm kind of mixed up. Who's behind all this? How is your sister Carla involved? I think you can tell me."

"Why does everybody pick on me?" Doris wanted to know in a self-pitying voice. "I don't know anything about this. What Carla does is her own affair."

"Baby you made it your affair when you brought me that photograph. Since then, you've been in this up to your neck."

"No. I'm not responsible for what Carla does."

"Well, I've just appointed you responsible. Until somebody better comes along. Somebody like Carla. Where is she?"

Doris passed slim fingers through her dark hair, her large eyes looking up at Reid.

"I don't know. I'm not my sister's keeper. She's free to come and go as she wishes."

"Nobody's *that* free. Come on, you must have some idea of where she's at!"

Impulsively, Reid seized her wrist.

The girl paled. "OH. Are you going to beat me up, like your girlfriend?"

The question seemed one of almost idle curiosity.

Reid released her wrist. He didn't get his kicks from beating up girls. Besides, from what she said, Lisa had tried it and it hadn't worked.

"I don't want to hurt you, Doris, but you've got to tell me everything you know. My life is at stake. A man can become pretty desperate under those circumstances."

"Ask Carla! She'll tell you what she wants you to know."

"She doesn't want me to know enough."

Doris met his eyes. "I can tell you nothing that Carla does not want me to tell you."

"How do you know Carla doesn't want me to know everything?" he coaxed. "She and I are very close, you know. Were—we're lovers."

"You lie!" Doris glared at him. "Carla would never betray me like that."

At last, a sore point, a chink in the armor to work on.

"But we have been lovers, Doris. Carla has a mole on her left hip. A small brown mole. How could I know that if we hadn't been intimate?"

Doris flung herself at him, her nails searching for his eyes. "You devil—you *raped* her!"

He caught her wrists easily and held her without effort.

"Maybe Carla gave herself to me willingly, or maybe I did rape her. I might even rape you if you don't tell me everything about this."

"You'd find out," Doris spat at him. "You'd find out more than you want to know if you went to Carla's apartment now." A wild look came into Doris' eyes. "Of course, you don't know where that is."

"No." He released her. "No, I don't know where that is."

Of course, he had only left there hours before. He—had not expected Carla to wait around there for him forever once the sedative wore off, but Doris seemed to know what she was talking about—as if she had just spoken to Carla a few, minutes before and knew for certain what was happening at the place at this moment.

The banging on the door startled Reid like an electric current.

"What's going on in there, Miss?" a strange voice called. *"We heard screaming."*

"Who is it?" Doris called before he could reach her.

"Police, ma'am."

That figured.

"It's—nothing," Doris said. "I had a dream. I dreamed I saw a—a ghost."

"We'll have to come in and check, ma'am."

He didn't know why Doris should want to cover for him, but she had so far. Reid met her eyes. "Is there a back way out of here?"

Doris nodded. "It's—it's in the back."

That made sense. He headed for the back.

He found himself in the kitchen, all white and pastel and outside a fat window he saw something moving around in the darkness. Somebody with a flashlight. It was either a cop or a burglar and there wasn't much worth stealing around here.

Behind him, he heard the front door open and footsteps entering.

"We'll have to look around a bit, Miss."

This was it. Did he want to see the police yet? No, he didn't. If he stayed here, he would have to face them. Outside, in the dark, he at least stood some chance of avoiding them.

Reid opened the back door as quietly as he could and slipped into the cover of night.

They must not have been looking for Lisa's car in particular. There were too many people and cars coming and going from the building. Only his and Doris' loud conversation had attracted the police who must have been staked out on her.

Now, he crouched in the bushes at the corner of the house, breathing hard, smelling the wet green smell of outdoor plants, and trying to decide his next move.

A circle of light hooped around him.

Then passed on.

He was well concealed here in the bushes but he couldn't stay here forever. Especialy since Doris was inside with the police, and might very well decide to tell them of his presence.

The circle of light was moving on, around the house.

Reid left the protection of the bushes and headed for the front of the house and his parked car.

As he moved forward, he kept near the house, his shoulders scraping the siding, staying in its protective shadows.

Now, just a few more steps…

He turned the corner and stopped with the blinding pain of a heavy-duty flashlight glaring in his face.

"Who are you, buddy?" and authoritative voice demanded.

"Who the hell are you?" Reid snarled. Get that damned light out of my face. What are you doing, hanging around this building?"

"I'll ask the questions here," the flashlight-bearer said defensively.

"You a cop?" Reid ventured.

"I'm a policeman. Who are *you?* I don't want to have to ask again."

"I'm the building manager," Reid supplied quickly. "What's the trouble, officer?"

The policeman killed the light. "We're watching this place for trouble, that's all. Nothing to worry about."

"That MacNiter girl, maybe?" Reid asked.

"Maybe."

"Listen, she's always in trouble. I can tell you all about her. Why don't you come in and have some coffee? I don't get a chance to talk to many people. I can tell you all about the MacNiter girl. Come on in."

The officer moved back a few steps. "Thanks. But I'm on duty. Got to make my rounds."

The officer with the flashlight moved off.

Reid moved faster.

He quickly found his car at the curb, turned on the motor and pulled away.

Behind him, he heard the excited sound of a man giving orders.

*   *   *

The door to Carla's apartment was unlocked.

Reid took stock of the situation, then remembering what he had seen in movies, some of which he had written, he threw the door back flat against the wall to make sure no one stood behind it.

The room was darkened, but the strange hunting lodge atmosphere was the same as he had left it.

No, there was *something different*.

A heavy, sweet, entirely unfamiliar scent hung in the air.

A strange, strange odor.

It made him feel slightly nauseous and light-headed, it—it—

Something was *wrong*.

Reid started back for the front door. But it was a million miles away down a long, long corridor.

He looked at his feet slowly swimming through a sea of air. His feet were moving over something. Not the rug. But a weird, obscene design patterned on the floor. Somehow, the lines made a form unspeakably hideous.

The smell was growing stronger, it seemed.

But Reid didn't mind.

He liked this scent. He liked it very much.

He sat on the floor to enjoy it and slowly…he laid back.

*   *   *

Carla. Doris. Lisa.

They were in the strange room with him, moving through the air, green with the strange smell, their bodies pink and white and tan, their flesh moist with animal desire.

"You don't have to make any choice," Carla assured him. "Don't trouble about making decisions, thinking. Don't think. Just have us all."

"No. I can't," he realized. "I can't have you all."

"Why not?" Lisa asked him. "Aren't we pretty enough for you? I think we're pretty."

Lisa put her arm around Doris' shoulders and let her palm caress the other girl. Doris smiled appreciatively at her.

The weird fog was seeping into Reid's mind, clogging it.

"No," he said. "No, I can't have all of you here now. I mustn't. If I did that, I'd never want to leave here. I'd spend the rest of my life here, just making love to you, wallowing in complete sensuality forever."

"Is that bad?" Carla demanded, bracing her hands on her unclothed hips. "What more can you possibly want?"

"But it isn't *real*. None of this is *real*. I've been drugged. I'm laying in Carla's apartment unconscious."

Carla approached him. She rubbed her breasts back and forth on his chest. She opened her mouth wide and kissed him. Her lips and tongue were moist and alive. Finally, she broke away.

"There," said Carla, "didn't that feel real? What difference does it mean whether it *is* real?"

"There's a difference," he said. "It means something to me. I can't live my life out in a dream. And I might be tempted to do it if I let myself have all of you now."

Lisa and Doris closed in on either side of him, their bosoms pressing into his sides. Their hands whispered over his body.

"But here it will be better than real, my darling," Lisa said, her startling eyes looking up into his. "Here I'll never make the wisecracks that get on your nerves and I'll never argue with you or try to boss you around."

Doris' finger hit into his chest, urging attention. "Yes, and here I won't be *afraid*. I won't be afraid of you, or of anything you suggest. I'll do *anything*. You can work out things for all of us to do, and I won't be shy about it, or maryish. I'll be happy and gay and willing, all ways, always."

Carla came to him and pressed her body against the length of his, her arms encircling his neck, so she could press herself ever tighter against his yearning flesh.

"Yes, my darling, and here, I won't be vicious or sadistic. I know what you want. You don't want to beat women or dominate them. You just want sheer studied sensuality out of a woman. You want her to work with you in achieving new plateaus of sensual pleasure for the two of you to enjoy."

"You understand," Reid marveled. "No woman ever completely understood that before."

"We understand everything about you," Lisa whispered into his ear and nipped it slightly with her teeth. "All you want is sex. You know that's all you really want. Sex. You only work and buy clothes and a car so that they will help you obtain sex partners. You only eat to stay alive so you can have sex. Other things you do, you do only as a poor substitute for sex. Here you can have all you want, all the time, here, and only here. You'll never make out so well in the real world."

"That is true," he realized.

The three of them were on him, their arms encircling him, trying to drag him down.

"What does it matter if it isn't real?" Carla hissed at him.

"It matters," Reid said weakly. "It *must* matter…"

The heady fumes were very strong in his brain.

CHAPTER ELEVEN

Lisa stared at the men standing in her door. "Lieutenant Oslow," she said. "And Sergeant Grubb."

"May we come in?" Oslow made a smile out of the hard lines of his face.

"I—yes."

The two policemen walked into the living room of her apartment and took chairs. Their dark clothes and darker expressions didn't compare favorably to the light pastels of the room.

"We have a few more questions to ask you, Miss Tanner," Oslow began.

"I think I must have told you everything I know, Lieutenant."

"There may be just a few things you've left out," Oslow said. "For instance, we just recently learned that you paid a visit to Doris MacNiter which you did not see fit to inform us about."

"You never asked me about it before," Lisa said coolly. "What is it you wish to know?"

"If you had Doris MacNiter's address, why didn't you give it to us?" Grubb interjected.

"I didn't have it when you talked to me. I verified it by calling several MacNiters in the phonebook. The phone was still listed in the girl's father's name."

"Yes, we know," Oslow said. "But that is just one instance of your generally unusual behavior in this case, Miss Tanner. Frankly, we are beginning to think you are holding out information from us."

"Would I hold out on the men who are trying to bring Jace Reid's murderer to justice?"

"You might," Oslow said, "if you didn't want Reid's killer caught."

Lisa's face drained. "Why wouldn't I want the murderer caught?"

"There might be several reasons," Oslow said sharply. "Need I go into the most obvious one?"

"You—you mean to suggest," Lisa stammered her breasts trembling, "that I killed the man they found in the ocean?"

Oslow leaned forward, as if ready to pounce. " 'The man they found in the ocean.' A strange way to refer to the man you say you loved."

"The body was never identified as Jace," Lisa said quickly. Perhaps too quickly. "Maybe there's been some kind of mistake. I can hope, can't I?"

"Of course, you can hope that that body wasn't Jace Reid," the lieutenant said smoothly. "But I wonder if you are relying on more than hope?"

Lisa stood up, her hands clenched at the sides of her skirt. "What are you suggesting, lieutenant?"

Oslow leaned back placidly. "All I'm saying, Miss Tanner, is that you know more than you're telling us and you really should tell us everything—for your own good, if nothing else."

"How dare you, lieutenant?" Lisa demanded. "Why do you pick on me when those crackpots are running around loose, those weirdos who made all the telephone calls and who must have been the ones that killed Jace—why don't you go after them?"

"Then they *are* involved?" Oslow said excitedly. "Is that what you're telling us? Is that what you're admitting?"

"What do you mean—'admitting?'" Lisa almost screamed. "You make it sound like a confession. I don't know anything about them, except they were after Jace."

"The boys who like to beat up women, huh?" Oslow said excitedly. "You're telling us that they're involved in the murder. Well, tell us more, baby. I want to hear all about them."

"I don't know anything more about them," Lisa insisted.

Oslow jumped out of his chair, marched across the room and grabbed Lisa's arm with fingers like handcuffs.

"You tell me," he said. "You tell me about these sadists. You tell me what they do, how they do it, who they are. Come on, I haven't all day."

"Let go of me," Lisa pleaded.

"I've got to know this, Miss Tanner," Oslow said in a monotone. "If you know what's good for you, you'll start talking."

"Let her go, Frank," Grubb commanded. "Let go of her, Frank, or so help me I'll slug you."

The lieutenant met the eyes of his sergeant.

Then, slowly, his fingers uncurled from the girl's arm.

"It's for your own good, Frank," Grubb said.

The lieutenant started walking numbly towards the door. "We'll have further questions, Miss Tanner. Later."

They were gone.

Lisa straightened up, her calm, self-possessed self again. She straightened the lines of her knit dress, and checked her hair-do

And then she buried her face in her hands and sobbed.

*   *   *

Reid woke up, his hands clenched tightly into fists.

He breathed deeply. There was only a hint of the strange odor he had smelled on first entering Carla's apartment.

The dope-induced dream was gone with the scent.

He moved painfully. He had been on the floor, on the weird designs chalked on the floor. A pentagram, and other, more unfamiliar devices.

Climbing to his feet, he rubbed his stiff, chilled shoulders and looked about him.

He didn't really believe she would be there but he passed the stuffed wild animals and entered the bedroom. The bed itself was rumpled and empty. Carla was not there.

Reid rubbed his aching head. Drugged again. Life at the sanitarium. But what had this stuff been? He had never known anything like it. Something the mere smelling of which in a closed room could produce unconsciousness. It wasn't marijuana. He had smelled that a time or two at Hollywood parties. Opium? No, something even more exotic than that.

This had been his second experience with dope in a matter of days. It was lucky he did not have any psychological dependence on it. Perhaps having a woman in a fully sensualized dream was not any different to him. It was all the psychological difference between having a virgin and a woman of the streets, even though the physiological results might be the same.

His mind returned to the sanitarium.

He had tried to get information out of Dr. Inge there, but Carla had "rescued" him. Or had she merely prevented him from finding out what he wanted to know?

He hardly expected that Dr. Inge and his charming staff—particularly the hulking female giant, Barrie—would be expecting him to return.

He hadn't been able to find out what he wanted here—he had found only the remains of some strange ritual involving an exotic drug—but perhaps his return to the sanitarium would bear better fruit.

166

*   *   *

There it was—*Dr. Inge's Home*, sitting on top of the hill, like a green fly resting on a pile of manure.

Reid walked up the long flight of concrete steps, his eyes on the dimly lit entrance.

It would be fairly simple to take the back way, up the gently sloping hill, held back from spilling down on the sidewalk by cement walls, but he didn't think they would be looking for him to march up to the front door, not after leaving so hurriedly in Carla's car.

He walked across the wooden porch as softly as he could. The doorbell was considered for a moment, then he tried the knob. It opened under his grasp.

Reid closed the door quietly and proceeded down the hall to the lighted door, Inge's office. Would he be there? he wondered. And how were his eyes? Could Carla really have blinded him? She could have, but somehow he doubted it. He was beginning to think it had all been an act for his benefit.

He approached the door stealthily and flattened himself against the wall beside.

Slowly, he inched his head around until he could see into the room. Inge sat at his desk, poring over some papers. He appeared far from blind, and strangely little disturbed for a man who had just lost a "dangerous" patient from his sanitarium.

Reid decided.

He stepped through the door.

"Hello, Dr. Inge. I've decided to come back."

The doctor dropped the sheaf of papers he was holding onto the desk.

"Reid!"

"Oh, now you remember the name?" Reid said softly. "I thought you thought my name was Raft."

"Raft, Reid, very similar. Which was it, did you say? Well, I'm certainly glad you decided to return of your own free will, Raft. We can help you here."

"Sure, you can. Barrie can make a helpless drug addict out of me by shooting me up every day and you, doctor, I wouldn't be surprised if you didn't have more ideas for cute experiments than a concentration camp commandant."

Inge smacked his lips, and *tish-tished.* "Persecution complex, my dear boy. But we'll cure you of that. You'll soon learn that Barrie and I are your *friends.*"

"If I believed that," Reid said, "I really would be crazy."

"Now, now—we don't like that word 'crazy' here."

"If I was as sick as you bunch of degenerates, I wouldn't like mention of 'crazy' myself."

"You aren't here to argue with us, Re—Raft. Why don't you just return to your room and lie down."

"Have you been handing out that line about treating the 'sick' so much that you actually believe it?" Reid asked. "You know why I'm here—I want information. And keep your hand away from that desk drawer with the gun in it or I'll break your arm off."

"I can't give you any information you don't have," Inge bleated. "I told you, Mrs. Raft committed you."

"There is *no* Mrs. Raft, as far as I am concerned. There isn't even any Mrs. Reid. I want to know who the woman really was. Could it have been Carla MacNiter? Was her rescue of me just a little stunt to gain my confidence for some purpose?"

"I don't know what you're talking about…" Inge's eyes and fingers strayed toward the desk drawer.

Reid banged his fist on the desk. In the small room, it sounded like an explosion.

"I told you," Reid said carefully, "to keep your hand away from that gun. If you don't, I'll start breaking your fingers one at a time. I've had just about all a man can take."

Inge's composure broke down.

"Reid, be reasonable. You should know I'm not going to admit anything to you. I wouldn't admit that I allowed somebody without the authority to order you held here. That would open me to a charge of illegal imprisonment. I'd lose my license, this home, my whole career, my whole life."

"Inge," he said, leaning forward, palms on the desk, "I told you I'm getting desperate. You'll tell me what I want to know or I'll beat you within an inch of your life."

"Two wrongs don't make a right," Inge said quickly, shaken. "You didn't have to use force to leave here. If you come back and use force, it will be considered assault, even attempted murder. You'll go to jail."

"Doctor, I'm under suspicion of murder right now," Reid became aware of Inge staring intently over Reid's shoulder.

"Get him, Barrie," Inge blabbed, breaking completely. "Beat him, kill him."

"Inge, I'm not going to fall for a trick as old as—" Strong hands gripped Reid's throat from behind.

"That's it!" Inge shrieked. "That's it! Fix him *good.*"

Barrie's fingers were like a steel vice around his neck. Reid elbowed and kicked trying to get free, but it was no use. The fingers were tightening and the pain was worse in his chest than in his throat. The room was growing darker.

"You shouldn't have hit Barrie," the huge woman intoned. "Now I must punish you."

His hands braced on her forearms, Reid swung his feet off the floor and hung suspended. Then he brought both feet and all his weight down on Barrie's toes.

The big woman howled in agony and her fingers exploded from his neck.

169

Reid dropped to the floor, on one knee.

Barrie kicked him in the face.

Her crepe-soled nurse's shoe caught him high on the cheekbone and sent him crashing back on the carpet. The sight of a huge foot ready to stomp down on his face hung over him. Sluggishly, very, very slowly, it seemed to him, he rolled out from under the foot as it stamped down on the unoccupied floor.

Instinctively, he grabbed the gigantic foot and pulled on it, trying to throw Barrie off balance. He couldn't budge her leg—it was as if it were welded to the floor.

She kneed him in the chest and he went back down on the floor.

"That's it, Barrie," Dr. Inge called enthusiastically. "That's a good girl. That's a darling girl. That's my darling. Give it to him *good.*"

The big ox—the big cow, Reid corrected himself—lumbered towards him more energetically than ever.

Her last blow hadn't really hurt him—just knocked the wind out of him. He was getting his second wind now.

Before she could get to him, Reid jumped up and put everything he had into a right that caught her on the left breast.

She stopped suddenly and grabbed herself with both hands.

"That—that hurt Barrie," she said, tears in her eyes.

"You come at me again, Barrie," Reid said, "and you'll get hurt worse than that."

"Don't let him stop you, Barrie," Inge popped up. "You won't let him stop you, not if you're my girl."

The giantess took a deep breath, and plowed towards Reid once again.

Reid flipped her across the eyes with his fingers. She howled in agony, and turned around and around in circles, groping.

Somehow, she seemed pathetic to him now, even though she was capable of killing him with her bare hands.

"Get him!" Inge screamed. "Get him—or you're not my girl!"

Barrie looked out through a lattice of her fingers and came at Reid once more.

With one hand shielding her eyes—or one eye, he decided, remembering the black lens he had seen in the spectacles she had been wearing last time—her guard was gone.

Reid dodged the hand reaching for him and planted a solid fist right in the giantess' mouth.

She covered her mouth with both hands, almost as if she were trying to hold in the scarlet spurts gushing from her torn lips.

"I can't do it, Ingie," she mumbled thickly. "He hurts me. He's too strong for me…"

"You fool!" Inge spat. "You ugly, stupid fool! You aren't good for anything else—I thought your brawn was at least useful. I could put up with your hideous ugliness for that, but now, you've failed me, you mangy, stinking, sloppy old cow. I'll have to take care of this myself…"

Inge was reaching for the drawer with the gun in it.

Reid was too far away. He could never reach him in time. And this time, he didn't think Inge was just going to threaten him with it. He would jerk it out of that drawer and blaze away.

He couldn't reach Inge in time—But Barrie could.

With a low, hurt growl she launched herself at the doctor and pinned his arms to his sides before he could open the drawer.

"Let go of me, like a good girl now," Inge squealed in terror. "I'm sorry if I said something to hurt your feelings, baby. Just stupid little lovers' quarrel, my beautiful one. My…my…back—you're breaking my…"

Reid ran up to Barrie and began beating on her head with his fist. "Come on now, girl, let him go or you'll kill him. You'll smash him all up and he won't be able to move or talk or anything any more, Barrie!"

It was no use.

Reid snatched up a paperweight from the desk and began beating the seven-foot tall woman on the skull with it. Inside the glass ball a tiny snowstorm swirled around a tiny house at the whole scene was being washed out by amber fluid.

With each smash on the head, Barrie's grip on Inge loosened just the least bit until at last he slipped out of her arms and flowed stickily to the carpet.

Barrie was still standing, swaying slightly on her feet.

Reid sat down the paperweight and kneeled beside Inge. He was still breathing. Some ribs were broken, he was pretty sure. He would live if his spine hadn't been cracked or his spleen ruptured. Inge's mouth opened and worked.

"You'll be okay, Inge," Reid said. "Just take it easy."

Inge's lips formed into a sneer. "I won't be the only one who gets hurt. Carla is going to hurt you. She's going to hurt you where it will hurt the worst."

Was he out of his head, babbling? What did he mean?

Suddenly, Reid had a sickening feeling he knew what Inge meant, what Carla was going to do, or what she might be doing this very moment.

Reid ran towards the door.

Behind him, Barrie stooped beside the old doctor and soothed his forehead with her ham-like hand, cooing softly as she did so.

CHAPTER TWELVE

The doorbell of Lisa's apartment was insistent.

She knotted the belt of her robe. Could that be Jace back? Or those policemen returning for more browbeating questions? She sighed. The only way to find out, she supposed, was to answer the door.

Lisa tucked the lapels of her oriental black silk robe securely in her cleavage, bringing the probing fullness of her bosom into sharp relief.

She opened the door. And faced a tall brunet with a sullen expression on her sensual lips. The intruder slouched her agile hips against the frame of the door.

"Are you Lisa Tanner?"

"Yes," Lisa answered automatically. "Yes. What can I do for you?"

"You can give me satisfaction," the brunet said, "for beating up my sister."

"You're Carla MacNiter," Lisa ventured. "Yes, I recognize the resemblance now."

"Nobody is going to be able to recognize you, darling, when I get through with you."

"I don't intend to brawl with you, Miss MacNiter."

Lisa attempted to close the door, but the taller girl forced the door open, stepped inside and closed it herself.

"You were perfectly willing to brawl with my sister, weren't you?"

"I was almost out of my mind with grief, Carla—I didn't know what I was doing. Actually, I feel sorry for your sister..."

Carla's dark, slightly slanted eyes widened. "Why should you feel sorry for her? Why should anybody feel sorry for Doris?"

"I'd feel sorry for anybody who was your sister, Carla," Lisa snapped. Then she regretted saying it. There she went with the wisecracks again. They were always getting her into trouble.

"I suppose," Carla drawled, "that I should say that I feel sorry for anybody who is Jace Reid's girl friend. You're going to find out it just doesn't pay."

Lisa felt her face go cold. "What do you mean?"

"Jace hasn't been cooperating lately…"

"Jace is dead!"

"Don't give me that line, darling. We both know how very much alive he is, don't we?"

"No," Lisa said coolly. "I don't think you know how alive he is. I don't think he'd bother to prove it to you. He'd want somebody who was at least half-alive themselves."

Carla's color went away, leaving her makeup standing out starkly. "Oh, you're a real smart broad, aren't you? I bet you're a million laughs—on the lecture stand. But you must be real nothing in bed. I bet you just lay there quiet, thinking of something clever to say. That's how Jace describes you in bed—a brilliant conversationalist."

"You get out of my home!" Lisa yelled. "Get the hell out of here, before I throw you out on your can. I don't have to stand here and take that from some half-butchy slut like you."

"You're going to take a lot more than that from me," Carla said, suddenly very quiet. "Jace has to learn to behave himself and take orders. He can't seem to get that through his head no matter how much we try to beat it into him. So—we're going to have to make an example out of you. Maybe if we half-kill you, he will behave himself to keep us from finishing the job."

Lisa pushed back a strand of red hair that had fallen into her eyes. "You and who else?"

"Just me, darling," Carla said sweetly, "and believe me, I'm going to enjoy every minute of doing it to you."

In one supple motion Carla took off the black belt of her black dress and whipped Lisa across the face with it.

Lisa retreated in furious surprise. She had expected the taller girl to come at her with claws or fists, not to strike with a belt. Confused, she tried to cover her face and the exposed area of her soft, white breasts as the blows of the leather rained down on her.

The red haired girl fell back on the couch, her legs thrashing aside the lengths of the robe she wore, exposing her white thighs to the flailing belt.

One particularly agonizing slash spurred Lisa into action. She seized the end of the belt and jerked, pulling Carla down on top of her.

The two women struggled on the edge of the couch for an intense moment, then rolled off, spilling to the floor.

Carla lashed Lisa viciously across the face. "You've got this coming to you, dearie."

Lisa arched her body upwards hard, trying to throw off the taller girl, but Carla clung stubbornly, her hand striking out again and again, whipping across Lisa's face.

Her clothes half-torn from her, areas of pink flesh laying revealed, Lisa's hand darted about desperately, grabbing and digging into the soft flesh of the woman straddling her.

At last, one hand flung far out and brushed Carla's foot. Lisa's fingers clutched at the foot and twisted. The high-heeled shoe came loose in the red head's hand and instinctively she struck out with it.

The spike heel struck Carla just below the sweep of her dark hair. Her eyes rolled back and she slumped backwards onto the floor.

Lisa climbed to her feet slowly, went to the bar in the corner of the room to begin mixing herself a drink.

"You," Carla's voice said behind her, "you are really going to need a special lesson."

Carla held a needle-thin stiletto in her hand.

The front door banged open and Jace Reid looked in, surveying the scene, deducing the history of recent events from the condition of the two girls.

"Don't try using that knife, Carla," he warned her. "I've already beaten up one woman tonight."

Lisa looked at Carla squarely. "That puts you and me in the same class, Jace, and I'm telling her not to try using the knife."

"So," Carla said, "you've returned to protect your little Amazon. Lisa doesn't need it, not from you. She can take care of herself."

"Nobody can take care of a knife in the ribs, Carla," Reid said. "Drop it."

Carla held out the knife in her open palm. "You want it? You always took what you wanted from me. Go on—come closer and take it."

"I don't think I want to take it where you want to put it. Just throw it on the floor before somebody gets hurt."

"Why must some people always be trying to keep somebody from getting hurt?" Lisa complained.

"Sometimes getting hurt is the best thing for people—it teaches them a lesson."

"You have to be smarter than somebody to teach them a lesson, Carla," Lisa insisted. "And you aren't hardly smarter than anybody."

"Now you are getting positively unsociable," Carla said. "Please don't try to detain me."

Reid shook his head. "I'm afraid you just can't walk out of here like that, Carla. There are questions that need answering. There is a neck to be saved—mine. You're going to stay around and talk."

"Wrong," Carla said. "You couldn't be wronger. Now just back away from the door…"

"Jace," Lisa protested. "You can't let her walk out, not just like that."

"She can go," Reid said. "But how far can she get? The police are watching your apartment building, Lisa, and must have a description of Carla. I've been able to come and go a few times because the police aren't looking for me in the investigation of my own murder."

Lisa wanted to tell him something about what Oslow had said during his last visit, but now did not seem like the right time.

"The police don't worry me. Just you don't try to stop me."

Reid backed away and let her pass.

Carla MacNiter slipped through the door, a broad smile on her face, the thin knife in her fingers.

"You let her get away," Lisa said.

"I didn't want her to use that knife on you," he said.

"No, you were afraid of her. Afraid!"

He was hardly listening. "I'm going after her. Lock your door behind me."

"No!"

"Huh?"

"No," Lisa said. "You can't go after her."

"Why not?"

"She might kill you."

"I'll have to chance it."

"Oh, you fool," Lisa whispered. "You always did have more guts than brains."

"Lock your door," he repeated, and went into the hall.

He saw the swinging door on the entrance to the stairway still moving back and forth.

Of course, she might have set that door in motion just to throw him off the track while she took the elevator, but he decided to chance it.

He pushed through the door himself, and stood very still.

A clacking of high heels came from above him.

Reid started climbing.

He couldn't let Carla get away from him now. Somehow, she was mixed up in all of this, she could supply him with the clue he needed to straighten out his life.

He climbed faster and faster, first one flight and then the other, up and up, on and on.

How many flights in this apartment building? he wondered.

And then there were no more stairs.

He was in a little wooden structure, a one-room shack of some sort right in the big city. A shack that all the stairs inside ended up in. And the door was open on a rectangle of darkened sky.

He stuck his head out cautiously.

The stiletto suddenly was stuck quivering beside Reid's head.

"Carla!" he called.

No answer.

"Carla, you threw away your weapon. You missed. You have nothing to attack me with. You might as well face the facts—I intend to talk with you."

The only sound that came back to him was the whistle of wind fluting through the maze of television antennas on the roof.

A maze!

Of course. That was where Carla was hidden in the maze of the TV antennas.

He made his way cautiously towards the maze of antennas on the roof.

Reid was not as certain as he had sounded in talking to Carla that she had no other weapon left.

He prowled through the metal rods and frames.

It was more than a maze or a nest.

The antennas made a metallic jungle, a jungle lurking with dangers.

Strange—he couldn't see clearly through them, the antennas. At close range they covered each other and concealed.

A jungle, he thought again, where any second a beast of prey might leap out and—

Carla landed on his back, knocking him to the top of the roof.

Something cold and hard and metallic was twisted around his throat.

Carla had found a loose wire somewhere and was trying to strangle him.

The second time in one night that woman had tried to kill him by strangulation.

Carla was strong and athletic, but after escaping from the giant Barrie, getting Carla off his back was letting the many aluminum arms stab at Carla, forcing her off him.

He rolled over against the base of a large antenna, a simple matter.

In a moment, he tugged loose the noose of wire, but by the time he looked up Carla was gone again.

But she was still on the roof.

The open door to the stairway was in sight and she hadn't gone that way.

He did not intend to leave that roof without finding her.

The first step seemed to be to go back and make sure the one door off the roof was locked, so she couldn't leave until he was ready for her to leave.

He started back.

Just then, a tall wooden-runged ladder that had been leaning on the ugly gray shed protruding from the roof, tipped and fell towards Reid.

There was no escape.

He knew he could not possibly dodge aside in time to save himself from a skull-shattering contact with two hundred pounds of seasoned wood.

There was only one chance for him, and he took it. Reid ran toward, the ladder, catching it near its base.

He held it for a second, then tipped it over, letting it clash to the roof with thunderous impact.

One trick that hadn't worked.

Carla was up here, and now he was more determined than ever that he was going to find her and squeeze the truth out of her.

"Were you looking for me?" Carla inquired, stepping out of the shadows.

"Yes," he said.

"And now, you've found me."

"That's right."

Reid started moving towards her, his hands ready at his sides.

"You're a fool, you know," Carla said.

"Sure," he said. "Sure, I'm a fool, and you're the lucky one considering what's going to happen to you in the next few minutes."

"You are a fool. We intended to teach you a lesson and we still intend that. The best way to bring home with you, is not to bring it home on you. There are others."

"Lisa?" Reid quited. "You tried that once."

"I was the beginning." Carla said.

"What?"

"I was the beginning," she repeated. "There was more for Lisa—from the men. The men are with her now."

"I ought to kill you," Reid said simply.

"Go ahead. Kill me, beat me, tie me up—but every second you take with me means that the men are spending with Lisa."

"It's a trick," he said uncertainly. "It's a cheap trick you're using to make a break. There aren't any men with Lisa."

"You may be right," Carla said regally. "Then again, you may be wrong. Are you going to take that chance?"

Reid stared at Carla's face for a long moment, then broke and ran back towards the stairs.

CHAPTER THIRTEEN

Reid started to break down the door to Lisa's apartment, then at the last second remembered his key.

He unlocked the door and flung it open.

Lisa lay on the couch, almost as if she were asleep.

He approached the sofa cautiously, his nerves strained to the point of a silent scream streaming through his body.

He was close to Lisa, very close.

She was still. Very quiet.

Lisa opened her eyes and looked at him.

"Hello, darling," she said. "I've been having the strangest dream about you. And about me."

"It's no dream," Reid sighed, "it's a nightmare. But thank God, the nightmare wasn't as bad as I thought it might turn out to be."

He kneeled beside her and found her lips with his own. His tongue insisted as his hands sought the swells of her flesh. He was grateful, oh, so grateful for her.

Lisa.

His Lisa.

Her tapering thighs moved impatiently and her hot, wet lips and tongue answered his in their own language.

Her hardened nipples dug into his chest and her delicate fingers began loosening his clothes.

"I thought I'd lost you," Lisa whispered. "And now I've got you back. I'll be good to you this time. I've got to be very good."

He twisted his lips maddeningly against hers—and pulled away.

"I don't—have time," Reid said. "There's still Doris. I must find her."

"But where can you look for her now?" Lisa pleaded.

"I think I may know where," Reid said.

*   *   *

The drug.

He had to find the drug he had first experienced in Carla's apartment. He knew what it meant to him now. He *had* smelled it before. It had been at Kerry Blaisdell's party, one of the first genteel orgies he had found himself at when he first got to Hollywood. It was rare. Rarer than opium, heroin or marijuana. He didn't know the name for it, but Kerry would. The same as he knew the name of every dope addict, homosexual, lesbian and sensualist in Glittertown.

Kerry was a goldmine of information about every perversion and about every pervert. He would know where Carla got the drug if anyone did. As a matter of fact, he might have supplied it to her himself. Not that a successful producer like Kerry needed the money, but he enjoyed dragging people down to the same depths of sensuality as he enjoyed himself.

This was Blaisdell's street. He recognized the tall palm trees, with tops looking like bloated pineapples.

It was a quiet residential district just out of Beverly Hills. Blaisdell could have afforded something better, but he preferred spending his inheritance on drugs, women and boys, instead of the mere pad where he enjoyed them.

That was it. The 1920-ish Spanish villa that was still attractive, but slightly decayed, like Blaisdell himself.

He pulled into the off-street parking and braked.

The iron knocker thumped against the door with satisfying violence. Inside, he heard a sluggish stirring, broken curses and a burp.

Blaisdell was at home.

The door cracked open to reveal one ravaged, amber eye.

"What the hell do you want?" Blaisdell growled. "The Salvation Army mission is on the other side of town."

"I'm glad you have that information, Blaisdell. You look like you're going to have to use it soon."

"Jace Reid, you old son of a—! It's about time you came around. If I hadn't seen that movie of yours, I'd think you were some kind of repressed hayseed. What can I do for you?"

Reid shook off the soft, perfumed, pudgy fingers that whispered along his sleeve. "Not what you're thinking. I just want some information."

Blaisdell opened the door wide, revealing his short soiled body, clothed in bright, sweated pajamas. "Anybody can get anything out of me—if they're willing to pay my price."

He stepped in with the same enthusiasm he would into a pit of quicksand. Blaisdell's home resembled the lair of a rabid jackel. Indescribable filth littered the expensive Swedish-style modern furniture.

"How much do you know about drugs?" Reid asked.

"All there is to know, my boy. All I can tell you anything you want to know, and teach you many things you've never dreamed about knowing. Just follow my example."

Reid swept the room with his gaze, the first time the room had been swept in a long while.

"Yes. I'll be sure to do just that. There's one drug in particular that I'm interested in. I caught a whiff of it at that first party of yours I attended. It's about the most potent thing I've ever known, just a sniff of it blasts you right off."

Blaisdell's reddened eyes squirmed in their sockets.

"What drug are you talking about, Jace? There are a lot of 'em, you know. Can't expect me to name it off right away from just *that* description."

Instantly, Reid knew that Blaisdell knew what he wanted to know, perhaps even *why* he wanted to know.

"You certainly seem to be taking this well," Reid said quietly.

"Taking what well, Jace?"

"My coming to see you this way."

"What do you mean? I told you I was glad to see you, for God's sake. Why don't you sit down and take it easy."

"That shouldn't be hard for a man in my condition to do."

"Huh?"

"After all, I'm a dead man, you know," Reid said.

"Man, you must've been blasting off already! What do you mean you're dead? You mean, like *beat?*"

"You did know that, didn't you, Blaisdell? I mean like *dead*. Are you the only one in Hollywood who hasn't read or seen the news of my death?"

A tremor set up in Blaisdell's soft jowls. "Well," he said, moistening his slack lips, "it must've been a mistake, eh? You're *here*, aren't you?"

"And you aren't surprised to see me. How is that, Blaisdell? I came here looking for information, but I think

I've found more than that. You're part of it, aren't you? I should've known you'd be part of anything dirty or rotten in Hollywood.

"That's why the smell of the drug was the same at your party, and at Carla's apartment. You were the source of it both times, weren't you?"

Blaisdell backed away. "Okay. Okay, I procure dope, boys and girls, for whoever wants 'em. That's my racket—what of it? You aren't on the vice squad are you?"

"I don't know, Blaisdell," he answered softly. "I can become pretty much of a moralist when it comes to saving my neck. You know damned well that you can't go on forever—it's just a matter of time before they catch up with you, and you'll go to jail where you'll have to cold turkey off your dope, where there won't be any women, and where the boys won't want anything to do with a fat old man like you. It's coming, but do you want it *now* or *later*. It could be now if you don't do just exactly what I want you to do."

"I won't be threatened!" Blaisdell shrilled hysterically. "You can't come in here and intimidate me!" The red fire in his eyes died to a pink haze. "Anyway," he mumbled, "who said I wouldn't do what you wanted me to?"

"That's fine," Reid said. "Just fine. Now you tell me everything you know about Carla MacNiter, about her damned cult, and about this plot involving my alleged death. Start talking!"

"I'm not really involved at all," Blaisdell bleated. "I just supply them their drugs, you know, when they want to have an orgy or something. And I supply that old crackpot doctor over on Alvarado with the stuff he can't get through the squares. I knew you were alive because I was over at the sanitarium the other day when they brought you in—"

Reid stepped forward and grabbed the man by the cowl-like bag of his throat. "WHEN *WHO* BROUGHT ME IN?"

"I don't know! God's truth, I don't know! I just saw *you* there."

Reid tightened his grip. "Was it Carla MacNiter? *Was that who it was?*"

"Sure, that's who it was; yeah, that's who it was—just like you say, Jace. Carla, that's who, yeah."

He shoved the man away in disgust. "I suppose you'd say anything that I wanted you to say. You probably really don't know who took me in to the sanitarium. You'd tell me if you did—you haven't the will power of a chicken."

"Sure, that's right, Jace. I'd tell you if I knew."

"You *do* know something about the drug, though, the drug that was used at Carla's apartment for one of her orgies?"

"Sure, sure, it's an Indian drug. From India, you know. They use it in the temples over there. It doesn't have a name. At least, the priests won't tell it to Westerners. I call the stuff Nirvana."

"You sold some to Carla?" Reid demanded.

"Yeah, I sold some to that bunch. To Carla, and—" Blaisdell stopped talking.

"And *who?*" Reid said.

"I—"

"Are we going to have to go through just where you stand again, Blaisdell?"

Blaisdell flowed down into a chair that happened to be behind him, like rancid lard pouring into a bucket.

"No," Blaisdell said, "we don't have to do that." Blaisdell's fat, but rather handsome, hands secured a pencil and pad from a nearby table. Artistically, he designed a short passage of writing.

"Here's the name and address of the only other person I supplied Nirvana to. Anything else I can do for you, before you leave? Like sign over the deed to this house?"

Reid pocketed the slip of paper. "No, thanks, Blaisdell. I'll just go away now, and just leave you to rot in peace."

He pressed the buzzer to the left of the apartment door and glanced at the piece of paper in his hands. The name and address Blaisdell had given him was that of Judy Balcomb, a name he had never heard mentioned before. He pressed the buzzer again, impatiently. Then he heard footsteps approaching the door from inside the room. The door opened.

The sultry brunet girl looked up at him. "Yes?"

"Miss Balcomb, I presume?" he asked.

"Mrs. Balcomb. What do you want?"

"I'd like to talk to you about a mutual friend of ours." He paused, then continued. "Carla MacNiter."

The girl's eyes opened wide in astonishment. *"Carla?* I—I don't know any Carla!"

He could tell she was lying. "I think you do, Mrs. Balcomb. May I step in?"

She thought for a moment, then said, "Yes, yes, please come in." She swung the door wide and Reid stepped into the apartment. After closing and locking the door behind her, the woman grabbed his arm unexpectedly.

"How did you find out about—about me?" she questioned pleadingly.

"I'd rather not say, if you don't mind. The important thing is that I do know about your connection with Carla and her orgies."

"You aren't a—a detective, are you?"

He shook his head. "No, I'm not. Let's just say that I'm a man who's interested in learning more about your little social gatherings."

For the first time since he had entered the apartment, Reid took a survey of the woman standing before him. She was, he said to himself, not the type of person you'd expect to find connected with a group such as Carla's. Her soft, brown hair flowed down onto her shoulders with a Veronica Lake twist, and the flimsy white negligee she wore did nothing to conceal her lovely curves.

"What do you want to know, Mr.—"

"Reid. Jace Reid." He walked over to a comfortable-looking chair and sat down. The woman stood before him, waiting.

"Take it easy, Mrs. Balcomb, I'm not here to interrogate you. Just want a few answers to some questions."

She felt somewhat relieved. "For a moment I thought you might have been someone my husband had paid to spy on me."

"Your husband knows nothing about your—er, outside activities then?"

"He knows nothing. If he did, well, you can imagine what would have happened to me."

Reid smiled. "Uh-huh."

"Still, there are times when I think he suspects. That's why I thought you might have been a private investigator."

"Well, I'm not, so don't worry about it," he said. "Where is Carla, Mrs. Balcomb?"

"Forget the 'Mrs.' Just call me Judy." She sat down in a chair opposite him and crossed one delicious leg over another. "I don't know *where* Carla is, Jace."

"When was the last time you saw her then?"

"At the last meeting. I seldom see her other than at her meetings, to tell the truth."

"How would you go about finding her if you had to—immediately."

"I really—couldn't say."

"Are you sure about that?" he asked demandingly.

Judy got up from her chair and slowly walked towards him. "Why do you want to know where she's at, Jace?" She stopped in front of him and kneeled down by his feet. "What does it matter?"

Reid looked at the woman knowingly. "Personal reasons. How do you contact her?"

She moved closer to him and he caught himself looking down at her soft, creamy neck. The "V" of her negligee parted open still more, exposing a portion of her well-formed breast. She searched his face for a sign, placing her hand on his.

"What does it matter…now?" she asked purringly.

In one smooth motion, she leaned upwards and placed an arm around his neck. Their lips met, her tongue darting hotly over his lips. She clutched his hand tightly and moved it over her thigh. The straps of her negligee flowed past her shoulders and she bent his head to kiss her bare neck.

She moaned softly in his ear, biting the lobe enticingly, laying her body onto his, her hands lightly touching the nape of his neck. Her hot breath sent a shiver of flaming emotion through him as his hands responded automatically to the nearness of the female body.

This was all that mattered. This was all that counted. The woman, and sex. As long as he had this, that was enough. That was all that—He caught himself up short.

If he didn't get on the ball and get to the bottom of this affair, he wouldn't be around to enjoy sex or anything else. He would be locked up in a prison or an insane asylum probably, if he managed to escape with his life, which hardly seemed likely.

He pushed the impatient-hipped little brunet away from him.

"Sorry, baby, but I haven't got time for fun and games. Let's get back to the subject you tried to get my mind off—unoriginally but interestingly. *Where's Carla?*"

Judy opened her mouth to speak—a reply or a protest, Reid would never know.

The door opened and there stood a tall man wearing a rumpled business suit and a surprised expression.

"Oh, Mr. Reid, here's my husband now," Judy said.

"Harry, this is Mr. Reid. He wanted to sell us some insurance."

Harry Balcomb's lean, horse-like face colored. "I hope he has some himself—he's going to need it."

"Harry, whatever do you mean?" Judy fluttered. Reid turned his gaze toward the woman sharply.

Her words sounded so phony, so patently phony. He realized, then. Of course, she *wanted* it to sound like a phony act. She wanted him to suspect, to become violent. After all, she was involved in some sadism cult—she liked violence. And from the expression on her husband's face she was gating to be able to witness some very shortly.

Reid stood up. "I certainly do carry full protection myself, Mr. Balcomb. I think every man should."

"Well," Balcomb growled, "I surely am pleased to hear that!"

The tall man rumbled down on him like an express train with its brakes out of control.

Reid braced himself; he had been involved in more violence in the last few hours than any time since he had got out of high school. But there didn't seem to be any choice in the matter.

After dealing with the giantess, Barrie, this lean, lanky lout didn't impress Reid too much. He studied the lunge, stepped inside the man's reach and caught him on the point of the jaw with a right cross.

Balcomb's head snapped back, and his lean features assumed a hurt look of surprise. Reid let him have one in the stomach—his look of surprise turned to astonishment. Bringing his fist down on the back of Balcomb's neck, Reid wiped out all of Balcomb's incredulity and replaced it with peaceful contemplation as the bony body folded to the floor.

"He gets knocked out sometimes," the girl said breathlessly, "but *not* that fast."

"I've had practice lately," Reid said.

He walked over to her. "Now where were we before we were interrupted?"

"Please," she begged, "I *can't* tell you."

"You mean you won't," he said flatly. "Listen, your husband will be waking up soon. How would you like him to know all about your connection with Carla MacNiter's cult?"

"No! I—listen, I don't know anything about Carla. I don't know where she lives or anything. I think she's got a sister named Delores or something like that—that's all I know."

"What about other members of the cult?" he demanded. "Who is Carla's second-in-command?"

"I...don't know..."

Reid caught himself staring at Judy's white throat thinking...strange things, impossible things... She was aware of him staring, too. She seemed disturbed, disturbed in a way she hadn't been when she took the sexual initiative, or during the violence with her husband.

"Listen, Jace, I do know one name that might be of some help to you—if I give it, will you get out of here right away, fast?"

"Yes," he said. Somehow, he felt himself that he should go quickly.

She gave him a name and a place and he went out into the light of mid-morning.

He brought his car to a stop near the entrance to the playing field, got out, and walked through the vine-covered archway which lead into the park. A small boy carrying a baseball bat and a catcher's glove, darted past him brushing him in his anxiety to reach the area of ball playing. Kids, Reid thought. He remembered back to his childhood, to the days when he and some of his neighborhood friends would get together on an afternoon for a game of ball with the kids on the other block.

How many years ago was that? He tried to recall. Probably too many. Those were the days, though. Nothing but fun and good times. Not like now. No, not like now, he grimly reminded himself.

He stopped at a water fountain, took a sip of the refreshing drink, then looked around for his bearings. The man he was after was Big Jake Pazdan.

He stopped one of a group of boys who were racing down onto the playing field. "There's Jake Pazdan?" he asked.

The boy looked up at him, thought for a moment, then said, "I think he manages *The Tigers,* but I'm not sure. Yeah, I'll bet he's the one, alright. Them dirt bums. The *Tigers.*"

"Is he somewhere out there—with the team?" Reid asked the boy, indicating the wide expanse of playing field.

"Well," said the youngster, "if he manages them, he'll be over on the northside field practicing. Probably for our game tomorrow. They beat the heck out of us last—"

"Thanks," said Reid, and the boy whipped down the path towards his friends, mumbling what dirty bums them Tigers were.

Reid laughed to himself. Yeah, kids were still the same. Down with the other team. Especially the ones who beat you.

He made his way past a team of aspiring Mickey Mantles and headed for the north field. As he moved closer to the area of activity, he made out a hulking figure in blue sweatshirt and dungarees, cap on his head, coaching some of the youngsters at third base.

Reid walked up to the man and stood patiently in the background until he saw his chance to interrupt him.

"Where's Jake Pazdan?" he asked.

The other turned his head at the question and studied the man before him with something resembling a maddened scowl on his face. He stuck a tongue in his cheek, removed it, then said, "Who wants to know?"

"I do, any objections?"

Before the huge man said anything further, one of the boys stepped up and said, "Come on Mr. Pazdan, let's get going with some more sliding practice."

Reid grimaced. So this was Big Jake. He didn't think that he'd care to have him for an enemy, not with that 50-some odd inch chest of his and those burly arms.

"Just a second, Jimmy. This man over here," and he indicated Reid to the boy, "wants to speak with me for a few minutes. You run on and take over the coaching yourself. And do a good job."

The youngster beamed. "Gee, thanks, Mr. Pazdan," and he scurried off to take charge of the practice.

"Okay, bud," growled Jake to Reid, "you heard the kid. I'm the guy you're wanting. Now what's up?"

Reid took stock of Pazdan's muscular frame again and an idea occurred to him. He wondered if it could not have been Big Jake himself who had fished him out of the water near the docks and brought him to the sanitarium, the funny farm. Jake was certainly well equipped for the task, being built as he was, and it would have been no problem for him to do it.

Reid decided to work on this new angle.

"Want to ask you a few questions about Dr. Inge's Home," he said to the baseball coach.

"Whadda you asking *me* for? I don't know nothing about any sanitariums," answered Big Jake.

"I didn't say it was a sanitarium, Jake. How did *you* know?"

"Well, I—I, uh, just guessed that was what you were talking about. You know."

Reid stared the other straight in the eye. *"How did you know?"*

A bead of perspiration rolled down Jake's brow and he wiped it away with a soiled shirtsleeve. "Look, mister, I ain't got no gripes with nobody and don't know from Adam about nothing, so why don't you just get the hell out of here!"

Reid stepped in closer to the large man and grabbed his shirt, pulling the two of them face to face.

"Better keep your hands off me, bud," he spoke through clenched teeth. "Otherwise there might be some trouble."

"What do you know about—" but that was as far as Reid got. Jake shoved him away and in the same motion extracted a switchblade knife from one of his pockets. He pressed the little silver button on the handle and the gleaming silver blade zipped open, its highly polished surface gleaming brightly in the afternoon sun.

"Hold it right there, mister! You take a step further and you're going to feel this blade right between your ribs."

Reid did as he was told. It wouldn't do him any good to rush Jake anyway, warning or no warning. A man like Pazdan could crush him much too easily for his taste.

"Now you turn around and start walking towards that convertible parked near the hill," Big Jake ordered. "But watch yourself! Don't be a jerk and try something foolish. There's a fellow I want you to meet, whether you *want* to or not. Now, *get going!"*

Reid turned and started towards the convertible.

This was the chance he was waiting for, he thought. Maybe now things would start to clear up—after he had seen where Jake was taking him.

*   *   *

Down.

How much further could they go down? He lost count of the steps. Already noon had changed to twilight and they seemed to be going on towards midnight. But now, they could go no farther. There was a door.

"Open it up," Pazdan said. "It ain't locked. I trust people."

Reid turned the greasy knob and swung open the door. There was a dead cat laying on the threshold. It had passed the stage of wet rottenness into a state of dry mummification. The dust around it was thick and undisturbed except for a thin trail of footsteps leading to a keg and an orange crate, on which lay a well thumbed dirty leaflet captioned *Bizarre*. High up in the basement room a single, rectangular window admitted indistinct light which was then almost completely obliterated by tweed-patterned burlap. A rat scampered halfway up the gray cement wall, then fell backwards and bounced off Reid's shoulder, to land on a pile of yellowed newspapers and scamper away into the musty shadows.

"It ain't much," Pazdan said, "but I call it home."

"Do you take in roomers?" Reid asked, sarcastically.

"During conventions, wise guy. You think just because I don't have as much money as you that I don't have any class. Have a seat."

"The keg or the newspapers?" Reid asked.

"Just siddown and shut up!"

"How long do you expect me to keep quiet, Jake, forever?"

Jake turned his knife idly, letting it catch a stray quantum of light. "That might be arranged."

"Alot of people seem to be interested in keeping me quiet. I wish I knew what the hell you all think I've got to say. Believe me. If I knew anything to get Carla MacNiter or any of her stooges, *like you,* into trouble, I would broadcast it from the housetops."

Jake stepped closer. "You would, eh?" Like maybe telling how you were kidnapped at the point of a knife, huh?"

Reid smiled, but somehow his heart wasn't in it.

"Take it easy, Jake. I wasn't talking about our little social visit today. I meant inside stuff on the way the cult operates. I don't know anything about that; I'm completely in the dark."

"Well," Jake said, scratching his nostril, "I got to admire a man who admits his ignorance."

"Listen, Jake, all I wanted to see you about was to ask why you people don't leave me alone. That's all I want. Just you leave *me* alone, and I'll leave *you* alone. I don't care *what* you do for kicks…"

Big Jake's eyes became bright in the gloom. "I get my kicks okay. Did you see all those nice little boys on my team? Everyday I get to watch 'em while they shower, and I give 'em a little spank and send them out on the playing field. And then I watch while they get beaned by foul balls, crack each other with flying bats, and give each other the spikes sliding into bases. Yes, sir; there's nothing like the great American game of baseball."

"Look, Jake," Reid said, "I don't want to hear about any of that stuff. I don't care what you do on your own time, or at the cult meetings; I just don't care. Understand?"

"You're trying to trick me," Big Jake growled. "I know *you*, buster. You're *plenty* interested in what goes at our meetings. I know what your tastes are. You want to hear about how we beat naked girls with whips, and make them rub vinegar into the welts and hang them upside down by their heels. But you aren't going to get anything out of me!"

"Jake, I'm telling you once and for all, I don't want to know anything about the cult. I don't think it's very healthy for an outsider to know these things."

"Oh, you aren't exactly an outsider—not from what Carla's told me, anyway. 'Course, you aren't a real 'ee-nish-ee-ate', like me. I've been Guardian of Arms just outside the door of three meetings already."

Reid exhaled deeply. He had drawn a complete blank. Pazdan was so stupid that they had never even let him attend one of their orgies. All his "information" came from some fantastic word-of-mouth story that probably bore precious little relation to reality.

All he had succeeded in accomplishing was getting himself trapped in a filthy basement with a psychopathic homosexual gorilla with a razor-sharp knife.

He was beginning to feel depressed.

"Hello, hello, hello. What do we have here?"

Reid swiveled around to see who was calling from the stairs. A small man was coming into view from the ankle up as he made his way daintily down the steps. Finally Reid could see his bland, pink face with a few strands of rusty hair carefully combed over a scalp that would make a perfect landing field for butterflies.

"What *do* we have here?" the little man said.

"I thought you'd want to see this guy, Billy. This just happens to be Jace Reid, and you wanna know something— *he* came to *me*."

"My, you are a bumbling idiot, aren't you, Jake? Now you've let him see me." Billy put a finger to his lips. "You should've told me that he'd be here."

"Didn't I see you at the police station—" Reid started to say. Great, he thought. I thought Jake was stupid, but I've just let something slip that may cost me my life.

"Yes, that's right, Mr. Reid," Billy said. "You *did* see me at the police station when Lt. Oslow first brought you in to question you about the man who claimed you gave him the idea for raping and murdering that schoolteacher. I was the man, of course."

"You seemed to have been cleared," Reid said, uneasily.

"I was *released*. I had a perfect alibi for the night of the crime when they investigated. There was a brief psychiatric examination, but I was released as harmless. After all, I couldn't have killed that girl."

Reid let out a sigh of relief.

" 'Course not," Jake said, "I did."

Jace looked around the four, bare concrete walls of the room, then to the small, hard, marble eyes of Billy, and to the soft, phlegmy eyes of Big Jake, and finally to the silver spear of his knife. This was beginning to look like trouble.

*　　*　　*

Oslow frowned and examined the beautiful face and body of Lisa Tanner as well as he could through the expert cosmetic and green-knit dress. He always enjoyed a beautiful woman, but he couldn't help wondering what the hell this one was here for. After their last meeting he had never expected Lisa to voluntarily see him again.

"Well, Miss Tanner, I've been expecting you to drop around," Oslow said warmly. "Won't you come into the inner office?" He lead her inside, closed the door, showed her to a chair, and walked over to his desk and picked up a knife.

"Just what can I do for you today?" he asked.

"I've come to tell you something, Lieutenant Oslow," Lisa said. "Jace Reid is alive."

"Yes, I know. Another man was murdered and it was made to appear that it was Jace Reid."

Lisa's air of serene confidence shattered. "How do *you* know that, lieutenant?"

Oslow held the letter opener at each end with his index fingers. "How do you suppose I would know that the man who was killed was not Reid?" Oslow asked, tonelessly.

"I—I can't imagine," Lisa stammered.

The lieutenant tossed the opener on the morning's pile of unopened mail. "You underestimate police methods, Miss Tanner. No one can completely obliterate fingerprints—Dillinger tried, and he didn't make it. The body proved to be not Reid's. As for the rest, I've been able to see through a few things in questioning you and others."

"If you've seen this much, you should see that you've got to help Jace," Lisa insisted.

"I'll be glad to help him—all the way to the gas chamber," Oslow said. "Or help him prove himself innocent, if he is. It's not my job to decide that; I'm not a judge or jury, only a policeman. My job is simply to investigate and present suspects for trial."

Lisa jumped up from her chair, her hands clenched.

"But you shouldn't suspect Jace!"

Oslow sighed. "I don't know—when a man is connected with a bunch of sadistic sex perverts, writes a lot of stories about them, is being blackmailed for beating a girl half to death, and is running all over town while he thinks everybody thinks he's a corpse in the morgue, the corpse of a man so conveniently 'for him' murdered, I turn into a nasty, suspicious old cop."

Lisa turned around and rested her head against the cool, frosted glass of the office door. "Won't anybody help Jace? Won't *anybody help him?*"

*　　　*　　　*

Reid looked from one to the other of the two men in the basement room with him. Jake was taking a bit more of his interest, due to the knife he held.

Billy finally broke the silence. "Fortunately for us, Jake, Mr. Reid seems to be even more a dunderheaded idiot than you are. Coming right to us, admitting everything he knew. Good Lord, the man shouldn't be allowed to run around without a keeper."

"Yeah," Jake said readily. "We'll have to turn him over to old Doc Inge to take care of."

"Ah, I fear, Jake, that Mr. Reid left Dr. Inge slightly indisposed, with just about every bone in his body broken."

Jake's eyebrows lifted. "I didn't think our boy here had it in him."

"He didn't," Billy replied. "Barrie did the job on the doctor."

"Oh," Jake said.

"Reid beat up Barrie," Billy supplied. "Beat her half to death, Barrie claims."

Jake flashed Reid of look of new respect. "I don't want to tangle with him then! I'm glad I've got this knife."

"You know, I do think Barrie has the hots for Reid. He's the first man who ever put her in her place," the little man ventured.

"I got the idea for a really miserable death for our friend here," Jake said. "Let's turn him over to Big Barrie and let her rape him to death."

"Charming, charming," Billy said. "You show flashes of genius in the usual black murkiness of your complete imbecility. The idea has possibilities but also catches. We haven't the time for that. The Mistress wants to see you at her sister's. She is taking care of something that should have been done long ago. I'm afraid you will have to take care of Reid in a simple, primitive fashion. Stick your knife in his heart like a good boy, Jake."

There seemed only one sensible course of action for a real man to take.

Reid ran.

There wasn't far to run, in the filthy basement room, but he could at least stay out of the range of a hand-wielded knife.

He kicked aside the stack of mouldering newspapers and crunched his shoes over a pile of 45-rpm records.

"He broke 'em," Jake howled. "He broke my rock 'n' roll collection by the Ron Haydocky Boppers."

"Lamentable," Billy commented briefly. "Perhaps it would be a good idea to kill him faster for that, do you suppose, my boy?"

Reid plowed ahead thought the trash treasured by Jake's childish mind, stacks of Tom Mix comic books, a set of Sky Altitude Secret Manuals, a complete run of Famous Monsters of Filmland, smashing through, sending all of them flying into the dust and darkness.

"I'll kill you!" Jake screamed through his tears. "I'll kill you for that!"

And now Reid could run no further—he was cornered. Almost as if as a symbol, he saw the rat under his feet that fled in terror when they had first entered the room. The rodent shivered in terror. You and me both, Reid thought.

Jake ran head long at Reid, the knife in front of him, tears of rage streaming down his face.

Then almost without conscious thought, Reid stooped down, scooped up the terrified rat and threw it into Jake's face.

Big Jake screamed in shrill terror, dancing in a frenzy, slashing in all directions with his knife—like east and west across Billy's throat, and tripping and falling on the blade himself and lying still.

The rat scampered up the long stairway towards the light.

Reid didn't know or care whether they were dead. He knew where Carla would be now and he intended to find Lisa's car and go to the home of Doris MacNiter.

*   *   *

He slid the V-wagon into the suggestion of a parking place between two big Buicks.

In the flagstone patio, he quickly located 327½ on the left, and stabbed the bell button.

The door opened and Reid and Doris stood face to face.

Again, he felt the strong sexual attraction he had first felt when he had seen her at the door of his own apartment. It was remarkable how much she looked like Carla. At first glance. Then on the second, you could see they were completely dissimilar—the way they held their heads. And their bodies.

"You know who I am, Miss MacNiter," he broke the silence, "and you may guess why I'm here."

Doris' face was white. So was her dressing gown.

"I thought you were dead," she said.

"I want to talk to you about Carla. You can tell me what I need to know, Doris."

"No, I won't tell," Doris said in a small girl voice. "I won't ever tell!"

Doris turned and ran across the smallish living room and slammed the inner door—to the bedroom, probably—and he heard the lock click.

"Hello, Reid," Oslow's voice said behind him.

Reid turned to face the police lieutenant with relief, and yet, some fear. I'm startled, he told himself. Only that. A policeman always startles us. We all have enough secret guilt's for that.

"Lieutenant, it's a good thing you're here. I was assaulted and kidnapped, and this girl knows something about it, I'm sure."

Oslow's face was unimpressed. "I wouldn't be surprised. Well, let's talk to her." He stepped inside. "Do you ever read newspapers?"

"I saw one. I know you thought I was dead. Someone must have wanted it to look like that."

"Someone must have," Oslow agreed.

"I only escaped a few hours ago from where they put me, a place called Dr. Inge's Home."

Oslow held up a hand. "Well get to that later."

"Later they might get away."

"You might have thought of that a few hours ago. Right now, Miss MacNiter might get away. Where is she?"

Reid gestured towards the locked door tiredly.

Oslow went to the door and knocked.

"Miss MacNiter—Doris—it's Lieutenant Oslow. I'm here. We can talk now."

"Oh no, I'll never talk," the muffled voice said. "Never."

"You were going to," a second voice insisted, another woman's voice. *Carla's,* Reid realized.

"No, not really. You didn't have to come back. You shouldn't have come back."

"I'll always come back and make you do what I want you to do. You know that, don't you? Don't you? You know I can make you do whatever I want you to do."

"Yes…yes…"

"Yet you insist on trying to fight me, to wreck my plans. I'll destroy you for that. I'll smother you. I'll—"

Oslow motioned to Reid. "Give me a hand with this door. Put your shoulder to it. I'd say we'd better get in there."

The two men put their weight to the panel door and the bolt of the lock cracked. The door banged open and flung them into the room.

Curtains fluttered silently at the open window and Doris lay on the bed, sobbing but apparently unhurt.

Reid rushed to the window and stared into the night. Outside a couple of cars started up and from the other direction a motorcycle roared into life.

"Any of them could be Carla," Reid said.

"Or none of them," Oslow answered.

Reid continued to look out.

"I wonder where Carla might head," the lieutenant said.

"I wonder," Reid said.

He looked back into the room to see Oslow moving towards the bed. The policeman looked down at Doris.

"I think," Oslow said, "that it will be best for me to take you into protective custody, Miss MacNiter."

Doris lay on the bedspread, convulsed by a quaking chill, her teeth chattering in her head.

"Oh yes," Doris said, "protect me from her. Protect me from her!"

Reid turned the key in the lock, turned the knob, stepped inside, turned around, took his key from the lock, closed the door, put his key into his pocket.

Every movement was an effort.

The questions they had asked him, about his disappearance, about the identity of the corpse that had been mistaken for him, about Doris, about Carla, about everything, echoed inside his skull.

He had to turn them off somehow. He had to let life seep out of the air and sun back into his body. He…had… to…sleep…

"Ready for the party?"

His nodding head lifted and he stood up, easing his back from the closed door. His hand slapped out to the light switch.

Carla sat on the arm of the sofa, her delightful legs crossed.

"My God, Carla, they're looking for you. The police. They think you killed that man that was supposed to be me. Or that we did it together. Or something." He wiped his hand across his face. "Listen, I'm being followed. They must be watching this place. They know you're here."

"I have ways of getting in and out of places unseen."

"Disguise?" he mumbled.

"When people think you are one thing, it is easy to get past them as another."

"I get it. Blonde wig. They aren't looking for a blonde."

"Something like that."

"Carla, your sister, Doris, she's in the hospital…"

"I know, I visited her there."

"You couldn't have got out if you had!"

"Yes, I managed to escape."

"What are you here for?" he demanded in total exasperation.

"To take you to our party," Carla said.

Reid shook his head violently. "No. I can't leave here. We'd be seen, followed."

"They're only watching the building, not your apartment itself. And you don't have to leave the building. It's right here, two floors above you. You must come."

"Why?"

"You must. They can't start without you."

"They can't?" he said, his senses unfocusing.

"No," Carla said. "You are the Master."

*   *   *

Beatniks, he thought.

Beatniks. Guys and girls in black sweaters. Bongo drums. The guys had beards. Weird wall decorations. Grinning devil masks. Huge black bats. Beatniks, that was all.

They looked up one by two and saw him standing in the door with Carla.

A whisper slowly climbed from their throats. "Master!"

A young boy of nineteen, very tall and thin, ran up to him. Ran.

"Master, at last I meet you. I've come before but I have never been able to see you before."

"I've never been to one of these things before."

Carla laughed. "You have been here often."

"Why would I come to a place like this?" he demanded angrily.

"Why did you come this time?" she asked him.

A short, greasy fat man came up to him and pressed Reid's hand into his two soft ones. "Master, I can thank you at last. My life was wasted—wasted—before I read your books and saw that glorious motion picture of yours. You introduced me to the delights of pain and death."

Reid pulled his hand away peevishly. "No. No. I'm not responsible. I'm not responsible."

Carla's laugh tinkled at his side. "That's what the A-bomb scientists said about Hiroshima."

A slender blonde girl threw herself at his feet and hugged his legs, electric blue eyes gazing up at him in rapture.

"Master, Master," she cried shrilly. "You have come back."

"I tell you I've never been here before," Reid insisted.

"You mean I have only had a vision of you before, when I saw you here?"

Reid stepped back, pulled away from her, straightened his coat. "It must have been some kind of mirage all right, honey."

"Then I must be," the blonde cried joyously, "damned!"

"What?" Reid mumbled more automatically than in true surprise. His eyes were searching through the crowd for the quickest way out.

"I shall be punished for my sins of the flesh. I shall!" the blonde rambled on. "You spoke the Truth, Master. I shall be punished, whipped, beaten, until I have paid. I must pay!"

Curiosity and some sympathy for the girl seeped through Reid. "What have you done that's so bad?"

"I'm as bad as all the rest here, Master. All of us must be punished."

"But what have you done?"

The girl screwed up her blue eyes in pain. "Yes. I must tell. That is part of the punishment. Master, you don't know the things I have thought about. With men on the screen, with men on the street. And as if thinking weren't bad enough, at night sometimes when I'm in my room, I..."

"Wait; you mean all of you are here to be punished for sex?"

"Of course," a slender young man lisped. "If I can get the curth of thex out of my thythtem, think of all the creative energy I will have for my work!"

"You will punish us, won't you, Master?" the girl pleaded.

"Me?" Reid said. "You want me to beat you with whips?"

"Oh no," the blonde said. "Not now. Now you are a Vampire. The teeth of a kiss from you will see that we all suffer the living hell of the Undead forever!"

"You can't believe that!" Even as he said it, he knew they could. There were hundreds of cults in Southern California each of which firmly believed that their leader had some kind of supernatural power. It ammended his statement. "Why would you believe that?"

"Master," the girl said awesomely, "we have seen you rise from the dead. What more proof do we need?"

Reid looked to Carla for help. She was smiling knowingly, like a devil.

Carla stepped forward and lifted her hands. "Chosen Ones, the Master, Great Reid, has assumed the non-flesh of the Undead. You see him as you have always seen him, but you know his corporeal body lies in the morgue. He will carry this Damned Body through an Eternity of suffering. He can do the same for us! It is only just that we pay for our evil desires and deals with a living hell. Fall upon the Master, Chosen Ones, and receive the kiss of the Undead!" Carla turned to Reid, whispering, "You have the Power."

As the tidal wave of human flesh poured towards him, Reid realized it was quite a reasonable idea that he was a vampire. He would give them the kiss of death. Starting with the blonde clutching at him.

But something deprived him of her.

Something knocked her out of his hands.

Something was striking the other Cultists down, right and left.

This something was before him, this terrible creature of vengeance was right in front of him, and it wore a mask of more hideous lust than any other there.

It was the face of Police Lieutenant Frank Oslow.

CHAPTER FOURTEEN

"Pretty messy business, I guess, that thing over to Reid's building," Grubb said. He sat on the edge of the desk, drinking coffee from a paper container.

"Those damn sex perverts," Oslow said, his feet up on the desk. He looked very tired. Older. "They ought to throw the book at them. The ones that didn't get away."

"What makes them get that way, I wonder, Frank?" Grubb said.

"Whatever it is, it makes 'em not hardly human. They don't deserve to live."

"Maybe you're too hard on them, Frank. I guess it's like they say. They just are sick."

"They're a sickness," Oslow snarled. "They should be destroyed. Burned up, like a fever."

Reid sat across the room, warming his hands that were cold on the paper container of coffee he held.

"That look on your face, Lieutenant," Reid said. "I'll never forget it. Your lust was as bad as anybody's there, or worse."

Oslow swiveled around sharply. "You want to know why I'm curious, real curious, about sadism and sadists, Mr. Reid? Okay, I'll tell you. Two years ago my wife was raped and tortured to death."

Reid was too numb to react. "I'm sorry."

"I'm going to get the butcher who murdered my wife," Oslow said, "if I have to get every damned sex pervert in Los Angeles."

"You work at it too hard, Frank," Grubb said unexpectedly. "You beat a hophead almost to death trying to make him confess that he killed your wife two years back. Yeah, and you looked like you were enjoying it, Frank. You better be careful you don't become what you hate."

"The public is right, Grubb," Oslow said. "Some cops are dumb. Only a dumb cop would say a thing like that before a witness."

The uncomfortable silence ended with a knock on the door.

A uniformed man put his head in the door. "Lieutenant, they got a girl out here named Doris MacNiter. The boys say the doctors over at Mt. Sinai found her wandering around the corridors demanding to see you. Nothing really wrong with her, so the boys brought her in."

Oslow nodded.

A second later, a disheveled Doris MacNiter stood in the door, wearing the same dress she had been wearing under her dressing gown the night Reid had gone to her place.

Doris looked about the room, small, frightened, alone. "Lieutenant, I must say it fast. I must say it while I have the strength. You must imprison Carla. You must imprison me. Carla and I are the same person, and she is getting stronger!"

"I'll be damned," Grubb said. "A Jekyll and Hyde. A schizophrenic."

Reid said nothing.

Oslow nodded thoughtfully.

"But how could she get away with it?" Grubb demanded. "Couldn't people see that both Doris and Carla looked exactly alike?"

"But they were not twins, sergeant," Reid said. "They looked like two different people. Human identification is an inexact art. Take even people as famous as movie stars. I have friends who say they can't tell Robert Ryan from Rod

Cameron or Janet Leigh from Joan Leslie—even those two girls' names are alike. Or those same movie stars can go out in public and often no one will bother them because they are not quite sure. Any actor knows a slight change in a person, in his posture or walk, can let them walk by their closest friends without being recognized. Various impersonations are notorious—Hitler, Churchill, Montgomery all had doubles during the war…"

A knock at the door interrupted Reid.

Lisa Tanner swooshed in and hugged Reid. "Darling, when I saw you leaving your apartment with that woman, I thought I should tell the police downstairs."

Reid ruffled her hair. "Sound thinking."

"Can you figure out what logical motivation this girl might have had, Reid, in kidnapping you and killing that other guy? This Dr. Inge has confessed she hired him to make telephone calls to you and stand outside your door and talk about big baloozas—Excuse me, Miss Tanner. Policemen associate with criminals so much, we sometimes get to talking like them."

"I think I know what she was after," Reid said. "Too many people thought they saw me at the Cult meetings. *Somebody* was there, using my name. A double. Somebody who looked like me, at least compared to a newspaper photo. The MacNiter girl dealt in impersonation herself. It was natural she would think of a scheme like that. She wanted to use my name for publicity and prestige value. She wanted power—power over the lives and fortunes of the misguided people in her cult. But her dupe, the actor—my double—must have wanted to take over the show. She started planning his murder then, and replacing him with the real thing. This would be an improvement, making the Cult think that the Master had risen from the dead. I would probably have thought that myself after being fed enough of Dr. Inge and Barrie's dope. I would have believed anything they told me. But when I broke out, Carla decided to offer me a straighter proposition. She offered it the straightest when she said to me during the Cult session: 'You have the power.' She was offering to share her power with me, perhaps to help me convince the Cultists to turn over all their property to us. Vampires don't need money; just blood."

Lisa had been listening intently to what Reid was saying, her usually calm, lovely face working. Slowly, she walked towards Doris MacNiter.

"You're going to die," Lisa said to Doris. "You'll die."

"No," Doris whispered. "I don't want to die. That's what she wants me to do."

"Cut the act, baby. You won't get off on an insanity plea. Your plan was too cunning for that."

"No…"

"Oh yes. You'll get the chair. And I'll be glad. No woman can do to my man what you did and get away with it."

"It was her."

"It was you. All you. You and she are the same. I could kill you with my own hands."

Suddenly, Lisa's well-manicured hand blurred out and struck Doris across the lips.

"I could kill you right now for all you've done and no one would stop me or blame me."

Doris retreated, one hand to her face, her wet red lips soundlessly forming "no," her other fist clenched and held in the cleavage between her trembling breasts.

Oslow started to say something but Reid restrained him with a cautioning hand.

"Of course," Lisa continued smoothly, advancing on the shaking girl, "it doesn't matter whether I kill you now or you fry in the electric chair, burn to a crisp, sizzle—"

"No!" Doris screamed. "I didn't do anything. It was all Carla!"

"But you are Carla!" Lisa insisted.

"No, no, no. Carla is real. She's a real person, my sister. She's driving down into Mexico right now. Sometimes I think—I think that she and I are the same, but…"

Grubb shook his head. "The tricks the human brain can play."

"Sergeant, Lieutenant Oslow," Reid said. "Doris is telling the truth. She isn't a true schizophrenic, but Carla is such a dominant personality since childhood she's probably been trying to convince her that she is. That Carla is part of her, the dominant part. Doris would believe it to a point. The point of her death. The threat of death will release a man who's been in a catatonic state for twenty years so he can walk away from a fire. Lisa could put that threat of death into her."

Lisa frowned. "That's why you told me to do all that? But why couldn't you do it, Jace, or the police?"

"Because," Reid said, "to Doris here, poor kid, a frightening, dominant figure has to be a woman."

"Ye gods," Oslow said suddenly. "While we're sitting here, Carla is escaping. I'll put a call through to the Highway Patrol to pick her up. By the way, Miss Tanner, you're from back East, but out here, we use the gas chamber instead of the electric chair."

Reid and Lisa entered Reid's apartment quietly. "What was that you and Lt. Oslow were talking about, Jace?"

"Oh just man talk."

"Now it's time for some man-and-woman talk."

He took her and held her tight against him.

"Lord, Lisa, after all the twisted lives I've waded through, all the perverted sex I've fallen face down into, it's good to hold a normal, healthy woman, one I can share some good strong human experiences with."

"Yes, darling," Lisa whispered. "Shall I get our nice coil of rope now?"

"You and your jokes," Reid said gruffly.

Lisa pressed a wet cheek against his lapel. "They keep you from coming apart at the seams."

"I like it when you come apart at the seams," he said, fumbling with the buttons of her blouse.

His hands slid under cloth, and made a release. Moon circles drew up into stars under his palms.

"How—how did you know Carla and Doris weren't the same girl?"

His answer was muffled as his lips explored her throat. "When a man sees as much of two women as I saw of them, he can tell them apart."

Lisa was helping with the clothes now as they moved towards the bedroom. He let his jacket fall heavily beside the bed. And then they fell heavily across the bed.

He remembered back when they had to discuss such a thing as this, when it was sometimes given and sometimes refused, but after so many times, now all they really had to pass between them was a look, a gesture, a movement of the head. And somehow that made it more exciting. They had no doubts about each other, whether one was disgusted, unsatisfied, scheming or substituting for someone else.

The smooth curves of her legs were whispering against his, touching, going away, sliding along his. Her stomach muscles rippled against his. Her delicate hands glided up over his shoulders, to grip them tightly and force his chest down harder against her thrusted, pointed breasts.

He slid one hand under her neck and felt the mass of the red swirls of her hair. The other hand he moved along her body.

His mouth closed over her salty, quivering lips as they opened to him.

Waves of sensation beat at them until the tide washed them away like castles built in the sand, and left them on the beach of peace, near the sea of death.

"Filthy hypocrites!" Carla screamed, standing in the bedroom door.

Reid looked at her in the doorway, black-suit, whip in hand. His reactions, his responses were dulled and slowed.

"You!" Carla shouted. "You call me bad because you say I killed and robbed and drove my sister mad. And you do *this*. Punished! You must be punished!"

The mad woman lashed at them with the blacksnake whip she carried. It bit through the sheets and into their flesh.

Reid did not ask himself how Carla had eluded the police, how she had gotten here. He only had time to think that in Carla's hand the whip was a deadly, lethal weapon and that was how she intended to use it. He had only time to think that before the lash struck again.

With an uncontrollable cry of pain, Reid rolled off the bed, onto his jacket. Lisa screamed as Carla's whiphand raised again.

Reid rolled over with the .32 Police Positive in his hand and shot Carla between her breasts.

Carla dropped the whip and clutched the wound to her as if it were some prize.

"I deserved it," Carla said. "I deserved it…"

And she slid down the wall and died.

Reid looked at the gun in his hand. Oslow was pretty smart. He said he might need it if he ran into any more fanatics from the Cult.

Lisa sat up in bed and tried to keep her face steady. "She was right. She did deserve it."

Reid shook his head. "Nobody deserves to die like that, but it was kill or cure."

Reid looked at the lovely face of Carla, peaceful for the first time in death, no longer seeking power or punishment.

"Kill or cure," he said. "And in the time I had left, I couldn't cure her."

THE END

Printed in Great Britain
by Amazon

47487348R00128